THE FIGHT IN THE AIR. *Page 42.*
    Our Young Aeroplane Scouts In Germany.

Our Young Aeroplane Scouts In Germany

OR

Winning the Iron Cross

By HORACE PORTER

AUTHOR OF

"Our Young Aeroplane Scouts In France and Belgium."
"Our Young Aeroplane Scouts In Turkey."
"Our Young Aeroplane Scouts In Russia."

A. L. BURT COMPANY
NEW YORK

OUR YOUNG AEROPLANE SCOUTS IN GERMANY.

CHAPTER I.

SAVED BY QUICK WIT.

"HOLD on there, I want a word with you!"

Billy Barry and Henri Trouville, the Boy Aviators, were in the act of climbing into a superb military biplane on the great parade ground at Hamburg when thus hailed by a mild looking man in citizen's attire, with face half-hidden by a slouch hat and a pair of huge, horn-rimmed spectacles.

There was a note of authority in that voice, gently tuned as it was, and behind those spectacles were a pair of eyes as keen as gimlet points.

The speaker was none other than Roque, the noted secret agent—"Herr Roque," if you please, fitting into his masquerade as a merchant having contract business with the authorities of the canvas city of aëroplane hangars.

"Come over to quarters for a few moments, young sirs, won't you?"

The polite manner of request was for the benefit of the bystanders, who had been awaiting the flying exhibit, but the slight gesture that went with the words indicated a command to Billy and Henri.

They knew Roque!

Heinrich Hume, aviation lieutenant, who usually had a good deal to say on those grounds, made no more protest than a clam at this interruption of a special aëroplane test. He simply waved two other aviators on duty into the machine, as Billy and Henri marched meekly away with the imitation merchant.

While many of the spectators marveled at the apparent breach of discipline, the lieutenant was content to let them wonder. At least, he offered no explanation.

Billy and Henri did a lot of thinking as they crossed the parade ground—there must be something brewing, or Roque would not have been so impatient as to invade the parade ground at the time he did.

Roque conducted the boys into Lieutenant Hume's private office at headquarters, closed and locked the door behind them.

Removing his spectacles, and throwing his slouch hat among the maps that littered a big table in the center of the room, the secret agent at the same time changed his form of address—the oily manner was succeeded by abrupt and stern speech, which showed the real man of brain and unlimited authority.

The secret agent had seated himself, without invitation to the boys to do likewise. They stood, facing the real Roque they knew by former experience.

"Where is Ardelle?"

Roque put the question like a pistol shot, and fiercely eyed the youngsters before him.

The point-blank query failed to reach the mark intended.

Billy looked at Henri and Henri looked at Billy, and then they both looked at Roque with never even a quiver of an eyelash. They had not comprehended what was behind the dreaded agent's snapshot at their nerves. The truth of the matter was, they did not know anybody by the name of "Ardelle."

So Billy, with a bold front, remarked: "You can't prove it by us, sir. Mr. Ardelle is not in our list of friends."

"None of that!"

Roque pointed a menacing finger at the astonished pair of youngsters.

"I have it beyond doubt that Ardelle was on these very grounds a day or two ago, and by the word of a man who could not be mistaken. Fool that he was not to be sure at the time, and only the garb of a sailor to mislead him."

Then it jointly dawned upon the minds of Billy and Henri that Anglin, the smiling secretary of the eminent director of affairs at Calais, and later in the rôle of a bubbling sailor here in faraway Hamburg, must be the Ardelle about whom Roque was talking.

They realized, too, that through their boyish delight in lending aid and a helping hand to one they had known in intimate association with that best of friends in France, they had unconsciously maneuvered themselves into a dangerous game, a slip in which meant a dance with death.

A tissue message from this very suspect that Roque was so eager to apprehend even then burned against the breast of Henri, a little wad of paper that now represented the price of the world to a pair of bright boys.

Condemned of mixing in the battle of wits between the grim Roque and his strongest wily rival from over the sea, and it were better that the young aviators had tumbled from their aëroplane during the last high flight.

But those who traveled in spirit with Billy Barry, the boy from Bangor, Maine, U. S. A., and his plucky teammate, Henri Trouville, in France and Belgium, can assure that it is no easy task to catch this pair napping.

The courage tempered by that first and continuous baptism of fire was good steel for any emergency.

Roque owned to himself that his quickfire had

failed to get results. His informant, himself just returning from a secret mission on hostile soil, had noted the movements of the sailor suspect on the aviation exhibit day, and also the attitude of Henri at the moment when the message was passed. But of the message itself, the reporting agent could have no knowledge. He was not near enough to detect a trick so deftly done.

Roque and Ardelle had measured brains many a time and often, but heretofore at long range, and the former had never seen the latter in person. Had such been the case, the French agent's invasion of the empire would have ended at Bremen, when these two masters of craft had both been guests at the same time of the same café.

Roque's unerring judgment had convinced him after the first question that the boys had no knowledge of the name Ardelle. Their first profession of ignorance was too real to be mere acting. The boys took care that the light that came to them as Roque proceeded did not shine in the direction of the lynx-eyed questioner.

The rigid lines in the face of the secret agent relaxed. These boys, after all, had once served him a good turn, with a skill, courage and fidelity far beyond the ordinary, and, perhaps, he was not sorry that he had apparently found them guiltless.

"Now, young sirs," said Roque, resuming the manner of the merchant, "I have another little journey in store for you. I don't know for certain that it will prove as exciting as the last jaunt we took together, when you located a shipload of guns for me, but maybe so, maybe so.

"After we have made our excuses to the lieutenant," he continued, "we will go over to my humble home in the city, where I have some new clothes for you. I do not think you are warlike enough to want to travel in any sort of uniform, especially with a simple tradesman like myself."

It was on the tip of Billy's tongue to ask Roque why he kept up that sort of talk with those who knew him without his mask, and when there was no purpose to be served, but Billy concluded that he had better let well enough alone.

A roomy carryall was in waiting at the further end of the parade ground, toward which the merry old merchant led his young friends, with a hand under the elbows of both. It was pardonable for the aviation lieutenant to grin when the trio were passing, after making their excuses.

It had not, however, occurred to Henri to smile a response. He was just then indulging in a cold perspiration, caused by a leaping thought that Roque might personally supervise their change of garments, and in that curious way of his light upon the tissue billet pinned on the inside of his (Henri's) shirt-front.

Because they had not fully understood the meaning of the dimly dashed message, Billy had suggested that they keep it for another sitting. The paper wad had not then turned into a torpedo.

Roque's house might have belonged to a retired gardener rather than to the man with the iron grip who claimed it as home. The dooryard blazed with red flowers, and the well-kept lawn was lined by earth beds spangled with blooms in colors beyond count.

"Welcome, young sirs."

Roque waved the way into a wide hall, at the end of which yawned a great fireplace. Bowing before them the boys saw the tallest man they had ever met outside of a sideshow, a very giant, who wore a long gray coat, with a good day's output for a button factory in front.

"This is my man of business, young sirs—Paul Zorn."

The "young sirs" instantly formed the opinion that Zorn would have no trouble in cracking a cocoanut between the row of glittering teeth he displayed when Roque so introduced him.

"We are going to put our young friends into store clothes, Paul. I hope you will be able to properly fit them, and it will also be my care that you do."

"Confound the man," thought Henri, "he has never since he called me out of the machine shifted his eye long enough for me to get a hand on that tissue, and now he's going to act as my valet. He's just full of suspicion."

Billy, also, had been figuring some in his mind just what would break loose if Roque should find the sailor's note in Henri's possession. All of the powers of argument this side of the North Sea would then avail nothing in the matter of convincing Roque that he had not been double-crossed.

The only crumb of comfort that Billy felt he could hope for if the drop fell was that Roque would quit his comedy acting behind the scenes for the once—but that was scant comfort, surely, under this cloud of anxiety.

The boys soon knew what Roque had meant by "store clothes," for it was a regular storehouse of the styles of all nations that the makeup magician maintained in the second floor back of his Hamburg home—uniforms galore, the garb of the fighting man in the Old World war, known under the folds of Britain's Union Jack, the Tricolor of France, the black double-headed eagle of Russia, the sable Cross of the German Empire; the attire of the dandy civilian, the sedate tradesman, the student, the clerk, the livery of house and carriage service, and, indeed, what not?

"A nice little collection, young sirs," observed Roque, which remark again prompted the giant Zorn to display his mouthful of shining molars.

"How do you think Paul would look in this outfit?"

Roque indicated on the display rack a regulation English uniform of olive drab, with puttees, and a cap of the traditional French arms shape, but of khaki color.

Even if the boys had been in the mood to say that Zorn would look like the Eiffel tower in any sort of uniform, Roque gave them no time to break in upon his humor.

"Nothing like keeping up-to-date, young sirs, in my business. It was only a few weeks ago that this new style French soldier first appeared in Havre. And here we can make his mate in a minute or two."

This cat and mouse play was wearing on Billy and Henri. Free of anxiety, they might have enjoyed digging into the maze of disguises as they would the pages of a popular detective story, but they had a play of their own to make, and no chance yet to make it.

"Now, Paul, how will we fix up these young flyers for a bit of ground work? Something plain, yet neat, I think, will do for the sons of Doctor Blitz—I am Blitz to-morrow, I believe, Paul?"

Zorn simply showed his teeth. He was not expected to answer.

"Now, my bird boys, get out of those uniforms and I'll make a pair of likely students out of you.

Do you prefer Heidelberg, the School of Arts, or the Conservatory? No matter, though, it is just a shift for a short journey, and I guess I can make you up to pass muster."

All the time Roque was chatting principally for the amusement of himself and Paul, his hands were busy sorting a pile of clothing and he was ready to start a couple of young Blitzes into society in the most finished style—from glazed cap to shiny shoes.

It was just at this moment that Billy was seized suddenly with a fit of laughter, and his high glee was directed at Henri.

"Won't you set 'em going in that layout!" he howled.

With that he made a jump for his chum, as if to hurry the process of transformation. The playful effort commenced at the throat and scattered a few buttons. Henri resisted the attack, and for a second or two held Billy in close arm lock—time enough for the assailant to get a pin-jab in the thumb, and a wad of tissue paper in the clench of four fingers!

Roque viewed the antics with a frown of impatience, but the assistant of grenadier size roared his approval of the fun.

Henri was brisk enough then in taking off the old for the new, and by the time Billy commanded attention there was no occasion for worry.

Billy had swallowed the tissue!

CHAPTER II.

A STIRRING HOLIDAY.

To be rudely routed out of a snug nest in a feather bed at 3 o'clock in the morning—a morning with a real chill in it—is not a desirable experience for the average house-bred boy, and even such seasoned campaigners as Billy Barry and Henri Trouville were inclined to grumble when the giant Zorn yanked the covers from their downy couch and gruffly ordered them to get up and dress, and to make haste about it.

By the pale gleam of a couple of candles, and the slight warmth from a newly kindled fire in a white china stove, the "Blitz boys" made their toilets of the interesting characters they were to assume.

"What time is it anyway?" yawned Henri.

"I guess I'm not good enough in higher mathematics to figure it out for you," growled Billy, as he tussled with leather shoestrings that tied, he said, "seven ways for Sunday."

The voice of "Dr. Blitz" sounded at the foot of the stairway, in the lower regions of the house. There was no "young sirs" about it. The "good merchant of Hamburg" was on vacation.

"Crawl lively there, you snails," were the words that ascended.

"Wonder what tip he is working on now?" whispered Billy.

"You will never know until you get to it." Henri had before been impressed with the fact that Roque was not in the habit of springing until he got on the board.

"Good morning, Dr. Blitz," was Billy's cheery greeting to the man who was making hasty breakfast at a table drawn up before a crackling fire in a big brick cavern. He could not have testified from side view that it was Roque, so he took a chance on "Blitz."

Along with a gulp of coffee the imposing person addressed shot a remark in German over his shoulder, which Henri afterward explained to Billy was very near to profanity.

The boys edged into chairs at the table, but missed a round of muffins through staring at the "doctor."

The merchant masquerade was wholly outclassed by this new display of the make-up art.

Billy wanted to say "ring the night bell," but sheer admiration kept him silent.

Whether it was the combined effects of the steaming coffee, hot muffins, and a big black cigar that followed, or the silent tribute in the eyes of his young guests, it was, nevertheless, a speedily noted fact that Roque was thawing into more gracious manner.

"I suppose you know that it is only a few hours now until Christmas, and we must find some special way to observe it."

Billy and Henri could not get the straight line on Roque's remark, but later realized that the holiday was of the like they had never before passed.

With a cutting wind from off the icy flow of the mighty river Elbe in their faces, the boys followed their leader to the docks, where they boarded a small craft, evidently built for speed, which had steam up and manned for instant start.

The captain was the same who commanded the deck when the boys had accompanied Roque on a previous exciting excursion. This official, standing at attention, stiff as a ramrod, gave no visible mark of recognition as the passengers boarded the boat, but Billy could have sworn that he saw something like a twinkle in the captain's right eye when they passed the gangplank.

"No use asking where we are bound for," lamented Henri.

"Not a bit of use," agreed Billy.

They were out of earshot of Roque, whose tall form, in rusty black, was outlined in the dawnlight near the wheel of the churning steamer.

The first intimation of what was to be their next landing place came in the word "Cuxhaven," passed by one sailor to another. The talk was in rapid German, but Henri caught the drift of the conversation without difficulty.

"By George," he whispered to his chum, "Cuxhaven is the place mentioned in Anglin's message."

"You mean Ardelle's message," corrected Billy.

"That's right," chuckled Henri. "I forgot that Anglin had become the big noise. Yes, it's the very place," he continued, "and it's a great naval base."

"It's a safe bet that Roque never hits a trail that isn't warm. Take it from me," and Billy was in great earnest when he said it, "there is going to be something doing."

Billy's prediction chanced, in this instance, to be more accurate than are some of the forecasts made by professionals.

It was in a dense fog that Christmas eve when the little steamer ceased chugging in the wide mouth of the Elbe, and the harbor lights burned blue. The captain condemned the weather in no uncertain terms, but Roque seemingly had no care for aught but his thoughts, as he leaned against the rail, with moody gaze fixed upon the anchored ships and the dim lines of the city beyond.

As he had shaped, not long ago, the famous raid of the German fleet upon English seaports, Roque did not underestimate the ability of his great rival, Ardelle, to open the way for a counter attack. Ardelle was known by the secret service to be on this very soil—and, surely, for some big purpose. Minnows were not sent to stir up a pool of this size.

"But they'll find no sleepy towns to blow up here," said Roque to himself.

He was all for precaution, however, and his intuition was nothing short of marvelous.

When "Dr. Blitz" and his "sons" went ashore it was the foggiest kind of a Christmas morning.

A stalwart marine attempted to put the doctor through the question paces, but the real Roque whispered a fierce something into the ear of the would-be questioner that set the latter back-tracking in a jiffy.

It was a curious and remarkable fact, but true, that an hour after the eminent secret agent and his young charges had landed in Cuxhaven, Billy's prediction, "that wherever Roque is there's something doing," was verified. Every submarine cable connecting the fortresses of this coast sounded alarm, particularly high-keyed the frantic signal from Helgoland, the fortress island, thirty-nine miles away.

Roque dropped his doctor character like a hot potato when he learned the import of the flashes. He tossed his traveling case of surgical instruments into the first open doorway he passed, and the boys were compelled to run to keep up with his long stride.

Bombs were falling from aloft, exploding among

the shipping behind them, while in front one of the projectiles crashed upon a huge gas tank.

"The nerve of the devil mapped this out!"

The bitter emphasis of Roque indicated that he laid the blame of this unexpected invasion upon one head—that of Ardelle.

In the meantime, the fog-ridden atmosphere was riven by blazes of powder from the shore guns, trained upward, and the air squadron, Zeppelins and naval seaplanes, were leaping skyward to meet their kind in aërial battle.

Roque charged madly into the air station, dragging the boys after him.

A seaplane was balanced on the polished ways for the sweeping plunge.

"In the name of the Emperor!" he shouted, shouldering aside the men holding the poised craft. The same fierce whisper in the ear of the aviation lieutenant had effect identical with that upon the marine at the docks.

"Get to your places, you moonfaces"—this stern command hurled at the boys. Henri bounced into the motor section, Billy settled behind the rudder wheel, and Roque swung himself into the bow seat.

The long hull was launched with the snap of training, and with motors humming left the water without a wrench from its skimming start.

The Boy Aviators, certified masters of the air, were at their trade.

They had need of all their skill and daring that day!

"Set your course northwest," loudly ordered Roque. "Hit for Helgoland like a bolt."

"Look out that you don't hit something on the way!" shouted Henri from the rear.

The last warning was timely, if Billy had need of warning at all. There was peril in the foggy stretches.

The upper regions were literally lined with aircraft. No less than seven naval seaplanes had traveled in advance of the British warship invasion of the German bay. Having dropped all the bombs they could through the mist, they were in full return flight to the convoying vessels. Zeppelins and hostile seaplanes zigzagged on their trail, and other dirigibles and fighting craft menaced their retreat still further on.

Billy guided the seaplane he was driving to the higher strata in order to escape mix-up with the contending airships, but on the thirtieth mile recorded, Roque, who had constantly demanded distance figures, ordered a lower flight, and, the fog clearing, the flyers could plainly see on the waves far below the floating warcraft of the invaders— light cruisers, destroyers and submarines. The Germans were combating this array with aircraft and submarines, but so great was Roque's impatience to reach the fortified island that the motors were put by Henri to the limit of speed, and so that part of the conflict is not in the record of the Aëroplane Scouts.

Just off Helgoland, though, the boys had the shock of noting the crumpling of one of the British seaplanes and the end of a brave airman.

"There's no escape when death stalks you up here," sighed Billy.

"Ware away, boy," called Roque, when the seaplane hovered over Helgoland, "wait until they see the color of the bottom of the machine or we will look like a sieve before we light."

Billy "wared away," and with motors at half speed, the seaplane circled over the supposed most impregnable stronghold in the world, awaiting some signal of recognition from the fortress.

It was finally given, and Roque directed immediate descent.

On the ground once more, Billy and Henri relapsed into their dutiful service as "sons" and rear guards of the renowned "Dr. Blitz." The glazed caps had gone the way of the winds, but, as Billy put it, "we are still dressed up to beat the band."

The boys noticed that, barring a few skilled workmen and engineers, they were the only civilians in the streets that evening. They did not count Roque, for he might turn out to be a general, if occasion served.

The latter had a busy hour with the garrison

officers, while the boys had an idle one, with about as much activity as is allowed a hobbled horse. It was evident that "Dr. Blitz" held this island as a holy of holies, secret even to his "sons."

"It beats me," observed Billy, edging away as far as possible from the guard stationed to keep them out of mischief, "how those Britishers ever got by this place."

"The bigger question," asserted Henri, "is, if they got by, how in the world did they ever get back?"

"That's what Roque is evidently trying to find out," intimated Billy.

The boys, while puzzling over the problem of "get by and get back," were looking at the huge fortress so tremendously fortified and noting everywhere an uninterrupted view of the sea.

They also surmised that an alert garrison was ever carefully watching the waters, day after day, night after night, hour after hour, in order not to be surprised by the powerful enemy.

"I guess the fog helped some," was the conclusion finally advanced by Billy.

"And Ardelle somewhere behind the curtain," suggested Henri.

"Oh, go 'way, man; Roque has given you the Ardelle fever."

Billy just then caught sight of Roque bearing down upon them under full stride.

"Speak of the dickens," he exclaimed, "here he comes now."

The shadows of evening continued to gather, and here and there on the island lights showed like glowworms. Roque shook hands with his officer companions. He evidently contemplated leaving in the same impetuous way that he came, but evidently not by the seaplane route.

A little steam launch tugged at its holding rope, in readiness to dash away into the misty deep. Two men muffled to the throat waited the order. Roque, with never a word to the boys, directed them by gestures to get aboard, quickly following. The launch cut through the now pitchy darkness of the Helgoland waters. With the island lights no longer visible, there could only be seen the lantern in front of the little boat, and it was a dangerous speed to be making, when the helmsman had scant view of hardly a yard ahead.

But the man at the wheel was in familiar element, to him, and the scudding vessel never came to drift movement until a glimmering signal guided to the landing place, the name of which would have meant nothing to the boys if they had had the care to inquire.

This was Christmas night in the Bight of Helgoland.

CHAPTER III.

A THRILLING MOMENT.

UNDER oak rafters, festooned with dried herbs, and toasting their feet at the cheery blaze of an open, roaring fire, the boys regained the Christmas spirit that had been sorely subdued in the previous dismal hour in the wave-tossed launch.

The house that had thrown open a hospitable door at the bidding of Roque overlooked the bay, and its solid walls had resisted the storms of a half-century. Mine host, Spitznagle, had he been dressed for the part, would have come very near to the Santa Claus idea, and even as he was, some of the idea hung about him in a radiant circle.

He could not, though, have possibly trimmed a tree in manner more satisfactory than he decorated the big, square table in the center of the wooden-walled dining-room, within easy distance of that first-class fire. Sizzling sausages, small mountains of crullers, fragrant coffee, mulled cider, and such like in quality and quantity, indicated a royal spread.

Roque, who had been prowling around somewhere outside for a time, suddenly preceded a gust of sleety wind into the cozy interior.

The Christmas spirit had apparently conjured up

a bit of a kindly spell for him, as the iron man fitted into the scene with far less friction than the boys had anticipated, considering the mood of this driving force during the trying day.

"Snug haven, this, eh?" jovially queried the late arrival, as he spread a pair of sinewy hands over the inviting fire. "You're spoiling these youngsters, Spitz," was Roque's side remark to the blooming boniface, at the moment stirring some savory stew in a glistening copper pot. Mine Host waved a three-foot spoon in mock protest against the playful accusation.

"Nothing like that at all, my dear man," he declared in big bass tone. "I will not spoil but will cure these children of their hunger."

"Draw up, my hearties," urged Roque, setting example by dragging an oak bench alongside of the bountifully laden table. Billy and Henri jumped at the bidding.

"Where are the men that brought us over?" asked Billy, presuming upon the fact that Roque was in one of the rare periods out of his shell.

"Back, I hope, where they came from," briefly replied Roque. "Those fellows are hardy stock," he added, "and can see in the dark. Don't worry about them."

"Cuxhaven is some aircraft place, isn't it?" Henri put this wedge in the conversation.

"Perhaps it is," acknowledged the secret agent,

"and" (grimly) "it may soon return the upper-story visit just paid with a cloudful of warcraft that will start a general hunt for cover."

"Had you ridden often in airships before to-day, Mr. Roque?" inquired Billy.

Spitznagle muffled a chuckle by a slight fit of coughing when he heard the question, and muttered something to himself like "donner vetter!"

Roque turned a quick eye upon the fat offender, and then gave Billy a smiling look-over before he made response.

"I confess, young man, that I have enjoyed some lofty travel before I met you, but I am willing to admit that I could not teach you and that partner of yours many new tricks in flying the heavier than air kind of machines."

"How about the Zeppelins?" cried Spitznagle, who could no longer suppress a desire to show his knowledge of Roque's prowess as an airman.

"Hold your peace, Arnold," advised the secret agent, shaking his finger at the eager champion, "my business compels me to learn a little of everything, and it's all in a day's work, anyway."

The boys were satisfied that Roque's renown had not all of it been won on the ground. Spitznagle would have made a good witness to that effect if he had been permitted to speak.

While the tall clock in the turn of the winding staircase leading to the upper floor of the old house

was whanging the twelve strokes of midnight,
Roque and Spitznagle pledged the fatherland with
uplifted goblets, and Billy and Henri offered a silent
toast to the assured soft beds upstairs.

When the early morning brought no disturbance
of their inclination for a little longer time to press
the pillows, the boys sleepily guessed that Roque,
for once, was not in a hurry to dash into new territory. As the sun kept climbing, and still no summons from below, curiosity overruled napping, and
the young aviators decided to investigate the cause
of this unusual consideration of their comfort.

Halfway down the stairway their ears convinced
them that the place was not deserted, for a spirited
conversation in the language of the country was
in progress, accompanied by a clatter of dishes,
and the ever present cooking odor of sausage as-
sailed their noses.

Besides Spitznagle, shrouded to the rib-line with
his flowing apron, were three very short men and
an extremely long one. The latter proved to be
no other than the giant Zorn. Roque was nowhere to be seen.

The heavy host noisily hailed the late comers:

"Good morning, sleepyheads, and all this fine food
waiting for you, too."

Zorn gave his best wide-mouthed grin, and then
went on talking, in lower tones, however, to his
short companions.

Billy and Henri made a substantial breakfast, and in doing so, hardly felt the need of the constant urging of the boss cook.

They could not imagine what had become of Roque, and as nobody volunteered to tell them, they concluded not to ask any questions.

The boys observed that one of the short men, with a large head wholly out of proportion with his stocky body, commanded much deference from the rest of the party.

Henri learned from the drift of the conversation that this determined looking individual was Capt. Groat of Friedrichshaven, the great center of Zeppelin factories, and while the captain was not in uniform he had the manner of rank.

Billy was quietly advised by his chum what the talk was about, and wagered that the two strangers were airmen.

"When these fellows commence to flock together on this coast," he asserted, "you can figure on what Roque meant when he fixed a comeback to get even for that flying raid yesterday on Cuxhaven."

The boys had withdrawn to the fireplace, and had an opportunity to exchange comments and conclusions between themselves.

"I'd like to take a whirl myself in one of those Zeppelins," was the wish expressed by Henri.

"Our flying education has been sadly neglected in that respect," admitted Billy, "but, you know, these dirigibles are among the things made only in Germany, and we're just over, so to speak."

As the morning wore away, Zorn made some remark to Capt. Groat that had attracted the latter's attention to the boys lounging at the fireplace. The captain arose from the table and approached Billy and Henri with outstretched hand.

"You speak the German?" With the question he bestowed a strenuous grip upon each of the boys.

Henri nodded, and Billy confessed by blank look that he did not know the language.

"It is easy, the English," politely assured the captain, "and we will talk it together."

Billy brightened at this. He was not fond of hearing through an interpreter.

"I hear you are the great aviators, and for so young it is wonderful."

"Thank you, sir," was Henri's modest acknowledgment.

"It is with the Zeppelin I navigate," advised the captain. "You know it not?"

"Not much," put in Billy, "though we once dangled on the anchor of one, and another time I fell with a monoplane right across the back of one of your dirigibles."

"Yes," remarked Henri, "and if it hadn't been for that, there wouldn't have been any Billy alive to tell about it."

The captain showed a disposition to continue his

talk during the afternoon with the boys, but a new arrival of evident importance interrupted. This addition to the party was a much older man than the rest, wore a military cloak, and his long, gray mustache curled at the ends in close touch with his ears. As he stood at the end of the big table, now cleared of its cloth, and rested a hand, enveloped in a gauntlet, upon the shining surface, everybody in the room saluted. Over the shoulder of this distinguished guest the boys saw the face of Roque.

As if by signal, further increased by the hasty entrance of three additional numbers, the attending company ranged by equal division on each side of the table, and all followed the directing movement of the man at the head of the board in seating themselves.

Billy and Henri were the only bystanders, for though Spitznagle had not ventured to flop down upon a bench at the table, he perched himself on a high stool, completely blocking the door leading into the pantry.

One of the short men who had first appeared with Capt. Groat produced a capacious wallet, and laid out in orderly array a number of neatly folded papers which had been contained in the leather.

"This is the navigator detailed to determine air currents, sir," explained Roque to the chief figure, at whose right elbow the secret agent was stationed.

The man in the cloak fixed his gaze on the expert with the notes. The latter accepted this as permission to speak, and read in precise manner the results of close observation during a recent aërial expedition of Zeppelins, escorted by armed German biplanes, in the vicinity of Dover straits.

Henri's quick ear and thorough knowledge of the Teuton tongue put him in line of complete understanding of the report, and that it seemed preliminary to a proposed general raid of aircraft on territory with which he was well acquainted.

Billy's only satisfaction was in watching his chum's change of expression as the news sifted through the latter's mind. He could see that there was "something doing."

So intently interested was the gathering at the table in the reading, that the very existence of the youthful outsiders seemed to be forgotten.

"Good; excellent!" commented the chief.

"It's a game with double trumps." Roque held the affair at Cuxhaven as a choking memory.

"There'll be quite a fall of hot shot, I promise you, if we get started right." This was the prediction of Captain Groat.

His lieutenants from Friedrichshaven nodded their approval.

In anticipation of a telling counterstroke by their air squadron, the plan makers at the table puffed up clouds of smoke from pipes and cigars, freely distributed by the happy Spitznagle when the

lengthy discussion officially ended. In the added
hours, when stone mugs were passing among the
thirsty, night had fallen outside, and the benches
were turned to the glowing fire.

While Spitznagle was touching the tips of numerous candles with the tiny flame from a paper spiral,
the empty mugs were being removed by an oddly
dressed fellow, who shuffled around in carpet slip-
pers like he was tormented with a thousand pangs
of rheumatism.

The boys had boosted themselves to good lookout points on the wide window ledges, behind the
lively circle around the fire.

The leather wallet and the survey notes of the
expert air traveler lay separate and apart on the
table, just as they had when the reading concluded.

Billy was idly watching the halting action of the
queer servitor, when, to the great astonishment of
the watcher, the apparent cripple, with rapid hand
movement, under cover of the wiping cloth he carried, deftly lifted and concealed the papers somewhere in the scarecrow garments he wore.

It was a tense moment. The word that would
have turned things upside down in that room trembled on Billy's lips. But one of those remarkable
instances of mental telegraphy checked the utterance. The man who had stolen the papers felt that
his action had been detected from an unexpected
quarter, and his eyes lifted to the very point of

danger. There was an appeal in the look—and something else, a flash of recognition that compelled a response. They were the smiling eyes of Anglin —or, as Roque would have it, Ardelle.

Billy, tongued-tied, saw the bent figure slowly shuffle toward the kitchen. He inwardly trembled at the thought of the stocky airman suddenly turning from the fireplace to seek his precious reports. He added another little shake in advance of the turmoil that was bound to be raised, anyhow, no matter how soon or how late the loss should be discovered. But the consolation of delayed discovery would be that Anglin had a chance to save his neck.

"What's the matter with you, pal?" Henri had just noticed that Billy was off color and wide-eyed as a trapped rabbit.

Billy, for caution, laid a finger on his lips. "I've seen a ghost," he whispered.

With a glance of apprehension at the group circling the fireplace, Billy leaned against the shoulder of his chum and with underbreath speed told of the presence of Anglin and the taking of the papers.

Henri was thrilled by the exciting story poured into his ear, and immediately took on his share of anxiety as to the outcome of Anglin's daring action.

Bursts of laughter resounded at the fireplace. The company was then applauding some humorous tale volunteered by Zorn, who had risen like a tower to impress the point of his story.

"Gee," murmured Billy, "will they never quit?"

"Don't fret," advised Henri, "the blow will fall in due time."

It did fall a few minutes later.

The main mover of the meeting was saying: "Gentlemen, it is nearing a new day, and there is great achievement before us. We go to prepare for it."

Benches were pushed back to clear the way, and this scraping sound had hardly ceased when the short airman, who had made the interesting report, hurried to the table for his valuable records.

The boys leaned forward in breathless suspense.

CHAPTER IV.

THE STOLEN PAPERS.

"My papers! The report! Has anybody seen them?"

The owner of the wallet shook it vigorously over the table, to assure himself that he had not replaced the records there, and then quickstepped the whole length and around the board, lowering his head again and again beneath the polished surface to see if the documents he was excitedly seeking could have possibly fallen on the floor.

"What's that?" cried Roque, starting forward. "You've lost the papers, you say?"

"I didn't lose them," almost shouted the airman, "they were left on the table, and if they're gone, they've been stolen."

"Hey, my friend," remonstrated Spitznagle, "we have no thieves in this house, and no enemies to the cause."

"This is no time to bandy words," roared Roque, "shut and bar the doors"—this last command directed at Zorn. The giant jumped at the bidding and sent the bolts rattling into their sockets.

The savage energy of Roque ruled all to silence.

Even the power under the cloak refrained from advising.

The secret agent dismissed suspicion as to the active participants in the conference, and as to the loyalty of Spitznagle he had not the slightest doubt. The trial horses must needs be two pale-faced boys backed up against a window-sill.

Roque, with his hands deep in his pockets, a habit he had when stalking a suspect, walked around the foot of the table and stood directly in front of the pair, fixing on them that gimlet gaze he used to terrorize.

Billy and Henri, when at bay, were the most keenly alive; their nerve always served them most in the supreme test.

They faced their inquisitor without an outward tremor; their previous anxiety was known only to themselves, and now admirably concealed.

Roque realized that he had no fluttering birds in his hands, and also was aware that a search of their persons was only required to acquit or convict these youngsters of the actual theft. He knew that they had not left the room, though why he had not long ago sent them upstairs to bed was a slip of mind he could not account for. But it had occurred to Roque that the boys had been in a position to see the table all the time since the company adjourned to the fire, and whatever had happened in regard to the papers they, if not the light-fingered chaps themselves, must have witnessed the perpetration of the steal. So he changed his tactics.

"Now, boys," he began with insinuating address, "there is a very ugly situation here, and as I have always heretofore found you dependable, cannot I now depend upon you to help me clear this up?"

Henri shook his head, in denial for both. "Search us," he said.

Roque, whose remarkable judgment of human nature has before been noted, felt in an instant that the suggested search would develop nothing.

"Who took the papers then?" he fiercely demanded.

"We were not on guard duty." Billy was inclined to resent this bullying, and showed it by his answer.

"Strip them," urged the short airman, who thought he, as the loser, ought to have a word in the controversy.

Roque waved the man away, and then abruptly moved to where Spitznagle was sitting, a picture of despair.

"Who was in the house to-night besides those now present?" was the question fired at Mine Host.

"Nobody but Conrad," assured Spitznagle.

"Who the devil is Conrad?" Roque fairly jumped at this information.

"Why, a poor crippled fellow, as queer in the

head as he was in the legs, that I had helping in the kitchen. He lost his job as cook on the coast line steamer *Druid* on account of rheumatism, and they sent him up here to me."

" 'They sent him up,' did 'they?' And now when did 'they' send him up?"

"About a week ago. But what's all this about Conrad you're asking, Roque? I'll have him in, and you can judge if he is worth a moment's notice in this kind of affair." Spitznagle started for the kitchen door, Roque at his heels.

"Conrad, Conrad," called Spitznagle.

"Conrad" had flown, leaving nothing behind him but his rheumatism and a dingy apron.

"Yell till you're hoarse, you fathead," raged Roque, "and the cows will come home from nowhere before you get an answer."

While Spitznagle was staring into vacancy, Roque stormed back into the dining-room and announced:

"We've been the dupes of that spy Ardelle. Nobody but he could have gotten away with a venture like this. But" (gritting his teeth), "I'll beat him yet. I say, Vollmer" (turning to the aërial recorder now minus his records), "you have the whole thing in mind and we'll strike while the iron is hot. We may outride the warning, for he can't get it flashed from this coast."

The man in the cloak came to the front on this

proposition. "The word is 'immediate,'" he proclaimed.

A speedy departure was in order, and Roque crooked a finger at the young aviators, bidding them follow.

"You are going to be mighty useful, my flying friends," he said, "and you'd better be." There was grim emphasis in these last words.

At noon the next day the boys were again tramping around after Roque in Cuxhaven. The character of "Dr. Blitz" was no longer in the play. Roque was trimly set up as an aviation lieutenant, and it was really wonderful how easily he merged into each part he assumed. "Students" no longer, Billy and Henri were happy in resuming their flying clothes.

"Best becomes our style of beauty," as Billy would have it.

There seemed to be some unforeseen reason for delay, as the aërial expedition did not start forthwith, as intended. Indeed, it did not start from Cuxhaven at all. It might have been that Ardelle's theft of the guide records had put a spoke in the German wheel, but as to that the boys could only hazard a guess.

It was on the twentieth day after the adventure in the house of Spitznagle that the young aviators again had the opportunity of operating a seaplane with Roque as directing passenger, and the uninterrupted flight brought them to the island of Amesland, for though Cuxhaven was counted as the airship base, it evidently was the intent to project the return attack on the English coast from the out-to-sea point before named.

What an array of the warcraft of the "upper deep"—the great dirigibles, seaplanes, destroyer, artillery spotter and scout aëroplanes. The boys were in their element. Even Roque had a smile for their enthusiasm. It was not the war spirit that animated Billy and Henri—they reveled in the show as airmen delighted with the life.

In this camp were none but the suicidally brave type of fighters, and it was only that kind fit to essay the trackless line of three hundred miles over the sea. From what the boys, or, rather one of them, Henri, could learn from the camp talk, a pair of the latest Zeppelin dirigibles were to participate, but the main movers of this attack were evidently to be airships of the small, non-rigid Parseval build, for bomb work. The truth of the matter was, the young aviators, at the order of Roque, were so taken up with the tuning of a seaplane just before the fleet went aloft that they could not have listed the starters with any degree of accuracy.

They only knew positively that they were going aloft, and their own machine would require their individual attention. About 8:30 that night the glare of a powerful searchlight from one of the

German airships directed its rays over the heart of the English city of Yarmouth. Two bombs dropped almost simultaneously.

The boys saw the city below suddenly plunged into darkness. Five more bombs were hurled from the sky. The fleet then swiftly moved northeast, and more bombs crashed into the town of Kings Lynn. Roque had assumed no active part as a leader in the deadly maneuvers—his was a thinking assignment. It was midnight when the fleet turned eastward and fled back across the North Sea.

"It might have been London," muttered the secret agent, "if the game could have been played without a break."

Preparations to repel just such an invasion had been made in the great city.

Ardelle must have gotten his warning across, but the coast towns failed to heed it.

The Roque machine kept its speed when the balance of the fleet checked flight at Amesland. The secret agent was bound for Cuxhaven, doubtless to plan another tiger spring at the foe. He was all for air campaigning these days.

"You will witness the sight of your lives, you young cyclones, before last night's mist of the North Sea dries in your hair."

This significant remark on Cuxhaven docks set the boys in the highest state of expectancy. It was seldom that Roque billed anything ahead of time, and surely something extraordinary must be in the wind.

Three days later, from a dizzy height, they witnessed a sky battle without parallel in military annals, and which dimmed the memory of any of their previous remarkable experiences in the war zone.

The French coast town of Dunkirk, to which the boys had on a happy day gone by been delivered by submarine and taken away in a seaplane, was the ground center of this spectacular conquest of the air—the first of its kind in the history of the world.

Twenty hours earlier a fleet of British seaplanes had bombarded the Belgian port of Zeebrugge, held by the Germans, news of which had soon after reached the mystery man, Roque, by way of one of the innumerable channels of communication with which he kept himself constantly in touch.

The German bird craft suddenly appeared over Dunkirk like a flock of gigantic sea gulls.

Explosive missiles fell as fiery hail upon the town. The tocsin sounded in the high tower of Dunkirk church, and the blue and white flag of the town was run up.

The roar of the fort guns, firing shrapnel, was heard, and all around the German fliers white puffs were bursting, as the pilots guided their machines in low-swooping spirals.

In compliance with the snappy commands of Roque, Billy circled the seaplane to every point of observation vantage, while the secret agent viewed the action of the armored Aviatik biplanes, dashing here and there with the sun glinting on their steel sides.

"Look there!" shouted Henri, rising and clutching a stay to preserve his balance. The air was clear, and the scene was open even to the naked eye.

Billy, at the wheel, risked a glance sideways.

A squadron of British aviators, encamped on the outskirts of Dunkirk, had taken the air to engage the raiders.

One speedy biplane darted straight toward the German craft. Henri saw the aviator clutch the levers of his machine in one hand and with the other unsling a rifle, beginning fire at a German birdman below him.

A half dozen armored aëroplanes of the raiding force swarmed in upon the daring Briton. His machine was peppered with lead, and it was apparent that the man had been wounded as he dipped toward the earth to evade the encircling Germans.

Other English aviators swept into the whirling combat, and to the rescue of their wounded leader. The raiders turned toward the north, now being shrapnelled by anti-aircraft guns stationed along the coast.

Roque pointed upwards, signalling for rapid ascent, and at six thousand feet the seaplane, with tremendous burst of speed, soon overhauled and outdistanced the slower warcraft, making a wide detour over the sea, thus avoiding the volleys of rifle shots from the Allies' infantry near Nieuport.

Roque, looking at his watch, turned to Billy, just behind him, remarking:

"That much in fifty minutes is not often recorded —of these things they shall sing on the Rhine."

In Bremen the boys paid grateful tribute to rest after the strain and stress to which they had been put by their relentless taskmaster.

"I feel," said Billy, "like the hump between my shoulders is going to be permanent, and I couldn't keep my elbows down to save my soul."

"If I could only get the whirr out of my ears, I'd be satisfied," was Henri's complaint.

It was not long, however, before the boys found relief from the kinks in their backs, and were ready and eager for the next move in their adventurous careers.

Just around the corner from their hotel was the very café where they had the thrill of seeing Anglin's face in the mirror while they were dining there with Roque.

"Wouldn't it be funny if Anglin were to bob up again while we are here?"

"I think, Billy, that it would be a tragedy if Roque had any inkling of it."

"Don't you hold the thought for a moment, Henri, that you could catch the Calais weasel asleep. Oh, I say, there's a concert on downstairs," quickly concluded Billy, as the notes of violin and piano were wafted above. "Let's hunt the music."

A high tenor voice was merging into the accompaniment when the boys reached the floor below, and they saw that the singer was one of the curly-lock type, and in evening attire.

What of the eyes, though, that gleamed upon the Aëroplane Scouts as they stood in the doorway—the artistic make-up could fool them, but there was no mistaking the smiling orbs under the blackened eyebrows.

Fox tracks were mixing again!

CHAPTER V.

WHEN THE LIGHTS WENT OUT.

THE vocal efforts of this new favorite had called forth round after round of applause, for good music never went amiss in Teuton territory.

Among the vigorous hand-clappers the boys noted a well-groomed man, apparently about forty, wearing an affable manner and the best clothes that the continent can produce.

Henri nudged Billy. "Size up Roque, won't you, please, and isn't he a dandy?"

Billy was first inclined to doubt the identity of their taskmaster, who a couple of hours ago was a far cry from being in the glass of fashion. Never before had the boys seen him in that sort of rig.

"You're dead right, Henri, it is the old scout. He's a corker, sure!"

This note of admiration had scarcely sounded when Roque was joined by a slender, wiry individual, also set up as a swell, with a shock of sandy hair, and sporting a monocle.

The fellow with the quizzing glass had apparently moved to get a better view of the singer, as well as to get in touch with the secret agent.

"Wonder if that's the man who spotted Anglin on the parade ground at Hamburg?"

"Don't let your imagination run away with you, Henri," advised Billy, who in speaking was careful not to indicate that his attitude was anything but careless.

The sandy-haired man was taking the same precaution, but Henri, nursing the idea that would not down, was more and more impressed with the belief that the elegant figure was seeking the measure and not the music of the warbler at the other end of the room.

If the singer had sized up the situation, it had not affected his rendering a bit of light opera that was just then exciting an encore. There was nothing at all the matter with his German or with his voice.

Nobody apparently was more delighted than Roque, and he appeared to be expressing his opinion to the wiry listener beside him.

The latter bowed politely and then sauntered toward the revolving door leading into the lounging section of the hotel, fingering a cigar as he proceeded.

Henri edged around nearer to the piano, the player of which was completing the program with a national air, the melody of many voices aiding the performance.

Billy had hardly realized the desertion of his chum

when he saw that Roque had changed his position, and was standing nearest the door leading to the street. The secret agent shifted something from his hip to the sidepocket of his coat, and Billy caught the glitter of that something in the swift movement. The boy guessed then that there was trouble brewing.

In the meantime, Henri, in an innocent sort of way, pushed still closer to the pianist, who was hitting the high notes in fine style.

As he passed within a foot of the singer, now idly posing, with an elbow on the piano top, he, without turning his head, joined in the triumphant chorus, but changed two words at the climax, and "beat it" reached Anglin's ear.

The French sleuth never moved a muscle, and it was as if the warning had been passed to a man stone deaf.

Anyone posted, however, would have known that within an arm's length of Anglin was a wall switch which controlled the electric lights by which the room was so brilliantly illuminated.

Billy had just had the experience of being rather rudely thrust aside by a couple of burly troopers, who seemed inspired to get as quickly as possible into the very center of the select circle.

"Get him!"

As this command rang out the astonished pleasure seekers started a panic, as if an alarm of fire had sounded. There was a rush for every doorway, but every way of departure was blocked by stalwart guardsmen.

Billy was not among those who tried to break through the doors—he was dodging among the charging force sent in by the loud orders to "get him."

Click! The room was suddenly shrouded in darkness, penetrated a little distance only by the lights beyond the entrance of the lounging room section.

The pursuing force, working from several directions, ran into one another's arms. The pianist, familiar with the place, leaped for the electric switch, and turned on the flood of light.

Everybody was present but the singer!

Henri had a perch on the keyboard of the piano, which he had sought to save a mad tramping on his feet.

"Set you to catch a weasel," sneered Roque, as the sandy-haired man stood staring at the shattered casement of the tall window overlooking an inner court of the hotel.

"He can't get clear away," retorted the sandy one.

"Stop him then," challenged Roque. "Don't stand there like a stoughton bottle."

The pursuers scoured the building from bottom

to top, and every street and alley roundabout, but it was a case of looking for a needle in a haystack.

Roque was in a black mood. Once more baffled by his cunning chief adversary, the only one he acknowledged in his own class, and on his own stamping ground—it was a bitter dose for the master craftsman.

Did he remember how he himself had spread a web over Britain, woven so finely that even Scotland Yard could not see it? Yet he rebelled at the like cut of a diamond.

"Stir your stumps," was his peremptory address to the boys, and they trotted to catch his long stride out of the hotel.

The sidewalks on both sides of the street were crowded with curious onlookers, attracted by the reported doings inside.

Roque bucked the line like a football star, and Billy and Henri followed in the cleared space without special exertion.

"He doesn't care whom he pushes," observed Billy, as he listened to angry protests along the line of travel.

Both of the boys were eager to talk over the latest disappearing act of that wonderful Anglin, but not so anxious as to take chances with Roque in earshot.

The secret agent turned into a silent side street, and stopped before a heavily grated door in the

gloomy front of a solid stone building that was a
skyscraper in height. Reaching through the grating, he evidently opened way of communication
with the interior, for in a moment or two a glimmer
of light splintered through the barred entrance, the
ponderous lock creaked, and the door swung back
on its massive hinges. A skull cap and a gray beard
showed behind the lamp shining in the doorway.
Roque pushed the boys ahead of him, and their
closing in was marked by a clang behind them.

They followed their guide through a long cor-
ridor and into a modern high-power elevator, that
shot noiselessly upwards. It was a circular room
into which they stepped, the very tip of a tower,
and a wireless telegraph apparatus was there in
operation.

"How is it working?" promptly questioned Roque
of an operator who was off his turn, and relieved
of his headgear.

The man jumped to his feet, all attention, and
replied: "There's been hardly a break for an hour,
sir."

Here was one of the hidden intelligence stations
that accounted in part for Roque's ability to get
searching and quick information. That he should
initiate the boys into his particular secret service
methods indicated a determination that they should
never get away from him.

As Billy said to Henri at a chance moment, "He

thinks we are booked for a life job as his air chauffeurs."

They were not aware as yet that in the extensive grounds, housed at the water's edge, was the seaplane in which they had recently traveled so far, and in addition a big biplane and two monoplanes were in hangars ready for service. Also the most speedy of steam launches rested at the private wharf.

Roque was a recognized genius, like every cog in the German wheel, absolutely thorough in his methods, and the means placed at his disposal were practically limitless.

Billy and Henri had climbed into the steep embrasure of a tower window and were enjoying the magnificent view spread out before them.

"How about my imagination now?" Henri was recalling exciting incidents in the hotel. "Didn't I get the figure of the sandy man as a spotter?"

"I think you did," admitted Billy. "But," he continued, "I didn't take much stock in the idea until I saw the revolver in Roque's hand. Then I knew that the fat was in the fire."

"I gave Anglin the cue to beat it, and I did the trick by breaking into that Rhine song," exclaimed Henri. "Yet he never made a move until the yell of 'get him,' and I thought the jig was up, sure. He's the coolest hand in the business, that fellow."

"Some of these days, maybe, he'll fall a little

short in one of those getaways, and that will mean
a tumble into six feet of earth."

"Not he," stoutly maintained Henri, "he's the
regular man with a charmed life. Say, I can't help
laughing even now when I think of Spitznagle calling 'Conrad,' and the expression on Roque's face."

Billy gave Henri a kick on the foot. Roque was
approaching with a sheaf of telegraph messages in
his hand.

"What are you boys jabbering about? I want
you to go down to the wharf with Albert and get
the seaplane in trim. I'll join you in half an hour."

Albert, a strapping youth, with the breezy way
of a sailor, guided the boys across the grounds to
the hangar, and watched with interest the making
ready of the airship.

"That's not my kind of a boat," he briskly stated,
"but I'll be bound if this kind of craft didn't give
us submarine workers a Christmas surprise. Ever
travel in a submarine?"

"We had a ride in one that we will never forget,"
replied Henri, as he applied the oil can to the big
motors.

Billy, busy with the steering gear, was not expected to answer, as he did not understand the question.

"It is all a question of ups and downs, anyhow,"
went on Albert, "bombs from above and torpedoes
from below."

This trade discussion ended with the arrival of Roque, who had severed himself from style and was again in aviation attire.

"Now, my carrier pigeons, you are in for a homing flight, that is, Hamburg; and it may be some time before you again get a breath of this port."

With this assurance the seaplane was launched and took the airline for Hamburg, leaving Albert to his own devices.

The travelers soon had sight of Zorn's everready grin at the home of "the well-known tradesman."

"We've been through a lot since we were last hauled out of these feathers," remarked Billy, as he bounced into the bed pillows that night.

Happily, "coming events do not cast shadows" for sound sleepers.

Roque had departed for the city before the boys charged into the breakfast room.

"He has gone to the store," announced Zorn, who uncovered his teeth an extra inch, in compliment to his own humor.

"Let's go over to see Lieutenant Hume," proposed Billy, after breakfast.

"Just the ticket," agreed Henri, "I'm crazy to get a peep at the old flying quarters again."

But Zorn objected to any move that Roque had not ordered.

The boys had to be satisfied with the prospect,

for to run against Zorn would be akin to tackling a mountain.

When Roque returned, sure enough, he was again playing the merchant—horn, spectacles, and all.

"Ah, young sirs, kindly waiting for the weary worker?"

"Same old blarney," muttered Billy.

Zorn chuckled as he relieved the "merchant" of his hat and overcoat.

"Some time ago I believe I told you that here you were only balancing on the edge of the great empire, and there might be an opportunity for you to see much more of the country. The opportunity is at hand. I have been called by trade interests further afield, and as I cannot consent to a separation, you will continue as my companions."

In his hour of relaxation, Roque really enjoyed this sort of word play, and he eyed the boys to see if they appreciated the fact that all of the best actors were not on the stage.

He was sure of Zorn's sincere appreciation. This man had seen the chief in many parts.

Henri accepted the cue, and, with a profound bow, and a hand on his heart, replied in kind:

"My dear Herr Roque, we would grieve if you left us behind."

"What of you?" Roque turned to Billy.

"Oh, anything goes with me." The boy from Bangor always hit straight from the bat.

The last evening of many in Hamburg was a very pleasant one to the boys. Roque's intimate knowledge of London and Paris was displayed in entertaining way, with no reference to his own exploits as the cleverest conspirator that ever invaded court and palace. He expressed regret that he had never seen America, and induced Billy to tell about Boston and Bangor.

It may also be recorded that with this evening the boys unconsciously said good-by to the character of the Hamburg merchant. They went far with the many-sided man, but never again saw him in the rôle imposed by this big city on the Elbe.

When the boys retired they left master and man —Roque and Zorn—conversing before the fire. With the coming of the morning, the journey to the unknown began, and the Aëroplane Scouts had no idea of its purpose or their assignment in the new sphere of action.

That it would, however, include further conquest of the air they might have guessed.

CHAPTER VI.

A FLYING VICTORY.

It was a great day for the boys when they set foot in imperial Berlin, with its palaces, art galleries, museums, parliament building, monuments, magnificent parks, and over all its martial spirit.

Roque, by which name, it might be mentioned, he was not known in this heart of the empire, soon demonstrated to his charges that he was the man higher up by his manner of getting about, and the high cost of living had no worries for him.

"Who'd have thought that we would be hitched up to a ten-time winner like this?" Billy was content for the time being to be allied with power.

Among the many who answered the summons of Roque in the intelligence bureau, the young aviators were most interested in a score of blond, blue-eyed, well-set-up Saxons, renowned as Zeppelin navigators, who were destined to guide the "terrors of the air" in furtherance of another raiding plan taking form in the fertile brain of the eminent promoter of trouble for the enemy.

While the boys had faith only in the heavier-than-air machines, they conceded that the risk taken

by the Zeppelin crews entitled the latter to brush
elbows with the crack flyers of the other kind of
bird craft. It was also true that when a Zeppelin
got anywhere it was a tremendous factor in war.
And it was no question but that the Fatherland
had gone Zeppelin mad.

Woe betide the hostile airmen who dropped the
bomb on the Zeppelin works at Friedrichshaven if
Roque had the means of catching them. It was
only another score that he had marked up against
Ardelle, whom the master agent of the empire
charged with planning this destructive performance.

"Roque said he was going to show us where these
gas cruisers grow," Henri advised Billy one evening, getting this news while his chum was engaged
in an argument with a Zeppelin worker.

"Something I've been wanting to see," exclaimed
Billy. "I owe something to a Zeppelin, even if it
is like a balloon."

This last was a sort of side swipe at the man who
had been on the other side of the argument.

"There is one thing sure, these dirigibles can't
camp out." This was Billy's first remark in Friedrichshaven.

He was peering into a big steel-framed shed with
a glass roof which housed one of these grim engines of the air—a great cylinder flanked by plat-
forms. This newest of the huge airships was about
the length of a first-class battleship, and the opin-

ion of the young aviator that it could not drop anywhere and everywhere like the aëroplanes he drove
was not a prejudiced one.

When Henri had a look at the powerful motors
he was impressed with their capacity to drink up
petrol at a most appalling rate.

"What's her top speed?" he asked one of the big
fellows who had traveled over from Berlin with
them.

"Forty-five miles in the calm," was the reply.

"Gee!" exclaimed Billy. "We could get a seaplane home for breakfast while they were waiting
supper on you!"

"Yet," claimed the Zeppelin expert, "it's the car
they're all afraid of."

"It certainly does look like a scaremark," admitted Henri, who remembered a certain evening on
the Belgian coast, when he was one of the company
aboard a stranded hydroplane dragged ashore by
the swinging anchor of a Zeppelin, which loomed
overhead like a cloud, and buzzed like a million
bees.

A gang of at least a hundred men swarmed about
the shed when the order issued for a trial trip of
the new super-Zeppelin, a sample of the fleet in
course of building, and Roque carefully noted every
detail of equipment.

The gas chambers were fed with pure hydrogen,

no common coal gas, and many thousand cubic meters were in the flow of this one envelope filling.

"Guess they'd have to carry a hydrogen factory around with this outfit to keep it going," observed Billy, as he noted the elaborate process.

"Not that bad," advised the man at his elbow, "this gas can be transported from the factory in cylinders under pressure."

"Just think of it," put in Henri, "I heard them say just now that it took thirty gallons of petrol an hour to buzz these motors."

"Biggest thing I know in the air business. I wish Captain Johnson could see an expense bill like this. He'd have a fit." Billy would, indeed, have counted it a red-letter occasion if his old friend, and the boss airman of Dover, were really at hand to take in this show.

To go aloft in an airship about which they were not thoroughly posted was a brand-new experience for the boys, but they were not in the least degree like the proverbial cat in a strange garret. It was easy riding, and none of the guns pointed their way. Billy carried a memorandum of a British military biplane, with a record of 10,000 miles, which Henri and himself had once patched up, that had been hit by 250 rifle bullets and sixty fragments of shells. He wondered if the immense craft in which they were sailing could have floated with, proportionately, about ten times that amount of lead poured into her. But Billy, of course, did not then know much about Zeppelins.

Roque, however, was eminently well satisfied, particularly with the improved method of distributing explosives where they would do the most harm. The airship had a special armored compartment for bombs near the propellers and a big gun mounted in front to destroy aëroplanes. "Get a fleet of these over the English channel," he proclaimed, "and somebody would think that hell had been moved upstairs!"

"I'll say this much," announced Billy, "I'd take an ocean voyage for my health if I knew when they were coming."

"But if the fighting crowd over there had the date and the hour, I'll promise you that the reception your fleet would receive would be warm enough to boil an egg." This was Henri's prediction.

"We never advertise," grimly remarked Roque.

When the Zeppelin had completed her trial trip and had again been housed by the small army of workmen, Roque informed the boys that he was going to give them the chance on the morrow to show their mettle in a biplane test, which was to decide the relative merits as to the speed of two special designs.

"I am going to put you up to jockey the machine that I favor," he said, "and, mind you, the aviators that will drive against you are among the finest in our flying corps. I always pick my men by personally knowing what they can do in any line of action. They seldom fail me, and it is with you to make good."

"We're going some, Herr Roque, when we come up to your standard," replied Henri.

"See that you are 'going some' at the finish of the race to-morrow," laughed Roque.

"It will be because something breaks if we don't hit the high mark," assured Billy.

"Go over and size up your winged steed," directed Roque, pointing to a hangar across the field. "Show them No. 3"—this to one of the attendants.

"This is no mosquito," announced Billy, after a view of the fine lines of "No. 3."

"Speed there, I tell you, old boy," was Henri's comment as he walked around the rigging, "and carrying armor, too."

In an hour the boys had fully comprehended all the new features of this up-to-the-minute machine. They had been builders themselves and knew a good stroke of the business when they saw it.

Returning across the field, Billy and Henri were introduced to the rival aviators by Roque. The German airmen were a jolly pair, and showed by the professional courtesy they exhibited to the two of their kind that the coming contest was wholly a friendly one, and the results to be of value to the flying corps.

"No. 2 is a little older than your machine," was the greeting of one of the Teuton experts, "but it can hold its own."

Roque, speaking for his champions, gaily disposed of this claim:

"Keep your eyes open to-morrow, Fritz, or you will get lost somewhere in the rear."

"No fear, sir; there are no cobwebs on No. 2."

"What are they talking about, Buddy?" asked Billy.

"They just think they are going to beat us, that's all," interpreted Henri.

A bright clear morning presented itself for the aërial race, and Lake Constance lay like a broad mirror under the sunlight. The course was set due north and straightaway for twenty miles, and the turn fixed at a high point called Round Top, upon which, Roque informed the boys, a tall flagstaff had been mounted.

There were no preliminary trials, for both machines had been carefully groomed, and each was as fit as a fiddle.

With the aviators up the biplanes scudded down the field for the rise, and got away upon almost equal terms, the German drivers slightly in the lead, through better acquaintance with the lay of the ground. They trailed a yellow streamer, while the boys floated a band of black.

The ascent reached 2,000 feet, when the machines

darted north like arrows. Roque and a group of officers about him followed the speeders through field glasses.

"They would run a swallow to death," remarked the secret agent to the aviation lieutenant at his side.

The aëroplanes had dwindled in the vision to mere specks, and there was no telling which was in the fore.

"Ah, they are headed back!" cried Roque. "Now for the show-down."

The glasses revealed the specks moving twin-like, and such was the terrific onrush that the crowd surging in the field soon caught a view of the contestants in growing size.

One enthusiast shouted: "Fritz will shut them out!"

But the glasses did not uphold the prediction. The machine with the black streamer was evidently using the reserve power that had been claimed for the newer make, and Henri was getting the best out of it. Yet the first-born craft was being handled in a masterly manner, had plenty of go to spare, and five miles still rolled between the speeders and the finish flag.

Now four, and the machines were bow and bow; now three, and the yellow band flapped a few feet behind the black; now two, now within the mile, and the whirring of the motors audible to the nerve-strained watchers below—then the close finish—

and the white-faced pilot crowned victor was Billy Barry of Bangor, U. S. A.!

When the aëroplanes made landing, Roque pushed through the crowd and favored the Aëroplane Scouts with a forcible slap between the shoulders.

The victors were quick enough to extend hands to the vanquished.

"My friend," cried Billy, giving Fritz a warm grip, "it was only fifty feet, and it was the new motors that did it."

Then the crowd cheered, while the efficiency committee agreed with Roque that "No. 3" was the machine to be many times duplicated.

"That was something over a mile a minute coming back, I guess," figured Billy.

"The fastest heavy craft I ever sailed in," was Henri's expressed belief.

"I think you youngsters could make a living here if I were to bounce you," said Roque, who had been talking to some of the factory chiefs. "But you are hooked to my train for a while yet. And that reminds me that the mentioned train starts in the direction of Austria in the next two hours. Vienna is not a slow place, you will find."

As Roque was likely to jump anywhere at the drop of a hat, the boys in his company had long since lost the emotion of surprise.

Perpetual motion had become a habit with them.

In the Austrian capital the travelers encountered many invalids from the front, men who limped a little, had an arm in a sling, or a bandaged head. The Viennese on the surface did not seem to be greatly impressed by the tragedy of the war—evidently becoming used to it—yet the determination to fight to the finish, while not as grim as in Berlin, was there, nevertheless.

Another thing that impressed the boys was that here foreign terms were still much in evidence—French and English. In Berlin it was different.

As Billy said, "we're in a better mixing town." He and Henri were told that quite a number of medical and art students from America had decided that Vienna was safe enough for them, but Roque kept his airmen close under his wing, and they had no opportunity to pass even the time of day with any of the U. S. A. crowd.

They had no present desire, however, to attempt a bolt from Roque and did not believe, anyway, that their detention was just then seriously affecting their health.

"Time enough to run," was Billy's philosophy, "when his nobs begins to kick in our ribs."

They were seeing plenty to keep them interested, the arrival of sleeping-car trains bringing the wounded to the capital, the movement of troops bound for the Polish or Galician front, the daily sights of the Ring and the Kartnerstrasse.

Roque, as usual, was up to his eyes in war business, ever behind the scenes but ever moving, for there is close military coöperation between Germany and Austria-Hungary. All interests related to the war have been pooled—one empire gives to the other what can be spared. The king-pin of secret agents from Berlin served a purpose wherever he went.

He sat in no open councils, but privately conducted many of his own, was constantly receiving and dispatching messages, and the devices he originated to aid his disguised subordinates burrowing for information in hostile territory were too numerous for detail. These latter operations were not accompanied by band music, for officially this live wire had no identity.

"If that man took a pot shot at the ocean you would never know in what direction he was aiming unless you happened to see the splash." Billy was not far from being right in the summing up of Roque's methods.

Within the next hour the boys "happened to see the splash."

A uniformed messenger handed Roque a telegram. The secret agent hastily read it, and sprang to his feet, his eyes aglow with triumphant satisfaction.

"I've got Mr. Ardelle in a stone box at last!"

CHAPTER VII.

THE RAIN OF BOMBS.

THE boys in silence watched the secret agent
as he further displayed his gratification over the
news conveyed in the telegram by snapping his fingers and slapping his knees, completing the performance by vigorous puffing of a big black cigar,
of which brand he always carried a plentiful supply.

Billy and Henri were just aching to learn more
about the reported capture of Anglin (Ardelle),
just where the "stone box" that held him was located, and how the "smiling sleuth" had happened
to run into a net that he could not break through.

But they were well aware that it would not be a
bit of use to seek the eagerly desired information
in advance of Roque's disposition to give it, and
they did not dare openly to show personal interest
in the matter.

It was not until the master plotter had burned
his cigar to inch measure that he thought to address the lads, fixing expectant gaze upon him.

"They jugged the fox in Alsace, on the way to
his home den, and filled up, I suppose, with some
choice morsels to regale the enemy."

"Maybe it's another case of 'now you see him and now you don't.'" It was Henri who plucked up courage to say this.

"Not this time," insisted Roque. "He is tightly in the toils, and never a chance to show his cunning. His course is run."

It soon became evident that the speaker proposed to be "in at the death," as fox chasers call the finish.

In less than two hours Vienna, the city gay and unafraid, was behind the three travelers, and their next goal the imperial territory of Alsace-Lorraine.

Into Lower-Alsace, on the last leg of the journey, Roque and the boys took to horse, with cavalry escort. They were again on real fighting ground.

Henri picked out of a conversation between Roque and the captain of the troop the words "Homberg castle," later that a group of important German officers resided there, and still later that within those walls Anglin was a prisoner.

Billy was immediately posted by his chum as to the situation.

Upon arrival at the castle, Roque, in that mysterious but effective way of his, established his footing as a privileged guest, and his first move was to pass the guard at the door of the strong-room, where his chief rival in the art peculiar was confined.

The boys without reprimand were close at the heels of the German agent.

Anglin was sitting on a bench, under the checkered light of a high, barred window. While his face showed harsh lines of great strain, the inevitable smile was in his eyes. He arose instantly from the bench, and bowed gracefully to the foe who confronted him.

"Monsieur, you are welcome." This to Roque. Upon the boys he bestowed not the slightest recognition.

Roque, not to be outgeneraled as a diplomat, inclined his head in return.

"I came a long way to visit you, sir," he politely stated, "and would have regretted had you felt otherwise than you have intimated."

This fencing with buttons on the foils was soon succeeded by the sharp points unprotected.

"Ardelle, the longer the breath is in you the more you can tell; is the breath worth the telling?"

"You speak in riddles, Monsieur," quietly replied the prisoner.

"Do you deny that you are Ardelle?" demanded Roque.

"Am I now on trial?" was the counter-question.

Roque extended a menacing finger. "Have a care, man!" he thundered.

The prisoner calmly ignored the growing wrath of his arch-enemy, shrugged his shoulders, and with a wave of the hand indicated that continued argument was useless.

"You will have until to-morrow morning to decide whether you will accept me as an advocate or an accuser."

The Frenchman turned wearily toward the window, and with his hands folded behind him stood watching through the bars the little gray cloudlets pushing their way through the blue expanse of the sky. It might be that this view would not concern him after the morrow. He was thus engaged when Roque stamped his way out of the room. Henri would have paused in the hope of one look from Anglin but the latter seemed wholly unconscious of the presence of the lads.

Under the steely exterior of Roque, the milk of human kindness had not wholly curdled, for he sadly said, half to himself and half to his boy companions:

"He must expect no more than I could expect; when we fail we fail alone, and so alone must we suffer."

It was about two o'clock in the morning of the day when Anglin, or Ardelle, was expected to read his fate in the eyes of those assembled as a military tribunal. The identity of the prisoner was, no doubt, fully established, for the boys had noted the presence in the assembly hall earlier in the night of the sandy-topped man who had started the hue and cry in the Bremen hotel, where the French sleuth was posing as a public singer.

Billy and Henri were tossing in uneasy slumber. The only sounds inside the castle were occasional snores from adjoining apartments and from the outside the whinnying and stamping of the cavalry horses.

Suddenly the quiet was shattered as if by a thunderbolt. The boys literally tumbled out of bed, gasping from the shock. A blinding flash at the windows and another crash.

Soul-shaking cries of "fire!" resounded throughout the building, and through the halls swept volumes of smoke.

The celebrated ancient furniture in the castle, it having been the summer residence of French nobility, was fine food for flames, and the red destroyer soon raged in conflagration.

Crash after crash, and with each concussion myriad sparks shot through great holes in the castle roof.

Bombs were being dropped from aloft.

The boys hastened with other occupants of the upper floors to the broad staircase in front of the structure. There they paused, elbowed against the wall by those pressing from the rear. There was no wild confusion or panic behind them, however, such as might have ensued under the same terrifying circumstances with other than trained soldiers involved. When Billy and Henri took to the wall at the head of the staircase it was a voluntary act on their part. The same thought with both had impelled the pause:

Had Anglin been released from the fiery vortex or still restrained by iron bolts and bars?

The room in which the captive was held faced a gallery running at right angles from the main stairway.

Pulling their jackets up and over their heads, the boys plunged through the wall of smoke on mission of rescue—a mission without result, for the door of the place of confinement was wide open, and no one was there.

The rescuing party of two then turned their intent upon themselves, and none too quickly, for they had hardly won safety when the castle enclosure was wholly enveloped by consuming flame.

Farm buildings adjoining were also ablaze, and the wide highway stretching away to the east showed whitely in the glare.

In the red canopy overhead winged shadows whirred and whirled, dipped and leaped.

Billy and Henri proceeded down the road to escape the growing heat and rolling smoke. When the roaring of the fire had somewhat lessened in their hearing, they detected a familiar hum, just ahead and closing down beyond the border of the rising mist of the morning.

As aviators, the boys were instantly aware that an aëroplane was working near and the proof was immediately furnished by the appearance of the aircraft itself, swooping into the circle of illumination, skimming close to the surface of the highway.

The lads sprang forward to greet the aërial visitor, and as they did so a tall figure, hatless and coatless, leaped from the cover of a ditch nearby, ran like a deer alongside the skimming biplane, and vaulted into the frame behind the daring navigator.

As the machine took the uplift, Billy and Henri were so close, and the fire-flow so vivid, that they plainly saw the faces of both the saver and the saved.

The man who had jumped into the machine was Anglin; the aviator was Gilbert Le Fane, the noted airman of Rouen, whom our boys had once followed in flight from Havre to Paris.

From the fire zone there was coming a hurrying body of men, and rifles began to spit lead at the swiftly rising aircraft. Too late, though, to reach the height attained by the biplane. A shrill yell of defiance floated back on the breeze of the morning, and deep and heavy were the expressions of baffled rage by those grouped in the road below.

Roque and the sandy-haired assistant could be heard above all the rest.

The boys were again in the rôle of innocent by-standers.

When the sun later replaced the flames in lighting up the sky, not a trace of the French airmen could be sighted, save the marks of their raid—the black-ened ruin of the castle and smouldering remains of the adjoining buildings.

Investigation instituted by Roque related solely to the escape of the prisoner. To put a quietus on his rival had drawn him from afar, and here again the elusive Frenchman had been jerked out of his clutches, this time into the very sky.

With the fall of the first bomb the single night guard over the captive had drawn the bolts that he might be ready to quit his post upon first order with the Frenchman in close custody. The second bomb so stunned the guard that he knew no more until regaining consciousness in the rear courtyard out-side. He could only account for his presence there by the belief that the man over whom he had held watch had picked him up and carried him out of danger. There was a back way that could be trav-eled, smoke hidden, without observation.

"But how about the aëroplanes dipping just at the right time and place to carry him off?"

This was the point that especially puzzled Roque.

A farmer boy, listening, open-mouthed, to the questioning, offered a solution.

"You see, Monsieur," he bashfully explained, "it

was a ghostly noise that was making between the
big noises, like the wind blowing through the neck
of a bottle stuck in a knot hole. I heard it in the
road, a long way."

It occurred to the boys that this distress signal
must have been given before they got away from
the roar of the fire, or while they were probing the
smoke in the gallery to reach Anglin.

"They were flying mighty close down and could
probably hear a howl like that, if they were listening for it and knew what it meant." This opinion was advanced by Billy.

"I don't much believe they could hear a call from
the ground, unless it came from the business end of
a gun." Henri was the doubter.

"It is no use to argue," said Roque. "The fact
remains that the air fellow had his bearings, and
he got the lead from somewhere. I am not giving
him credit for being a mind reader."

"That reminds me, Mr. Roque," remarked Billy,
"that we might test this gearing business by a little
air trip somewhere and soon."

"I have just such a thing in thought," grimly advised Roque, "and I will warrant that you will
hear a few ground sounds before the quitting minute. We are going to take a down look at Belfort."

Now Belfort is a French fortress, where the soldiers in red and blue had been finding security

every time they were rolled back from the plains of upper Alsace.

A tremendous amount of gunpowder had been burned on the flat ground in front of this stronghold, and our boys were in for a smell of it—something that would recall perilous travel with Colonel Bainbridge and Sergeant Scott in previous campaigns.

A wire to Friedrichshaven had started on the way the makes of biplanes that Billy called "Roque's best bet" since the day of the famous race over Lake Constance.

"Business will soon be looking up," joked Henri, when he heard of the order for the shipment of "No. 3's."

The presence of Ardelle in this region, extreme southwestern Germany, had raised suspicion in the mind of Roque that some special demonstration was brewing, and the lurid performance of the French airmen in blowing the roof from over his head served to further elevate the confirmed idea that trouble and the French agent always traveled together.

Roque was not here to mix in the actual military operations—that was not his business, but he was ever open-eyed on the trail of the boss gamester on the other side. He had expected this time to put his rival on the safe side of the ground, but spades did not prove to be trumps.

Somewhere in the gap of Belfort, as the valley south of the Vosges mountains is popularly known, Ardelle was, no doubt, preparing for another come-back, and Roque was scheming to meet him half-way.

There was no chance to get under the guns of the frowning fortress beyond the frontier, so the only way to size up the situation was to go over them.

Here was where flying experts jumped to the front.

CHAPTER VIII.

ALONG THE BATTLE LINE.

WITH the arrival of the biplanes from the factory, the Boy Aviators were kept busy with brief test flights over valley and plain, awaiting the convenience of Roque for the wider sweep he was planning. It developed that the boys were expected to navigate separately on this occasion, Billy to pilot Roque himself, and Henri to be accompanied by one Renos, who had been awarded a service badge of honor for his work as an aërial observer in giving first warning of the advance of a French division against Burnhaupt, which saved the day for the Germans.

"The seaplane is the rig for weight carrying," exclaimed Roque, in accounting for this assignment, "but these machines, as you know, are solely in the speed class, and it is many chances to one that we will be compelled to tax every ounce of power before we get through. So we have no use for deadwood."

Renos, who was to sit behind Henri, was the silent man of the expedition, as far as talking was concerned, but when it came to be up and doing he could be counted on to the limit. He was a hu-

man route-box of the Sundgau, the fighting territory, and very much at home in a flying machine.
When the two machines one morning flew over the
German frontier, in compliance with the "ready"
order of Roque, Renos' knees were crossed by a
wicked-looking rifle, and of the party he was the
only one armed.

Billy, observing this war-like figure, asked Roque
if he expected to get into close quarters on this
trip.

"Not unless some of the bomb-throwing crowd
that scarred the landscape the other night should
cross our path," replied the secret agent.

As Renos was the qualified guide, the biplane
bearing him went to the front, and Henri received
overshoulder directions as to the course to be maintained.

The apparent reason why the German expert did
not pilot the craft himself was that he wanted a
loose hand in case of emergency, and a free eye
for the panorama below. He was satisfied, too,
that one as good as the best was doing the steering.

Henri was instructed to keep a respectful distance from the near mountain peaks, where the
French had mounted artillery, for one round from
these guns, close enough, would have ended the
flight and the flyers there and then.

But Roque and Renos kept constant vigil with
glasses, and Billy wondered that the pair did not

get a crick in the neck with all the head-turning they did.

A sharp order advised the pilots to send the biplanes farther aloft, and circle. The French fortress of Belfort could be seen directly underneath.

The aviators well knew that an explosion close to an aëroplane is often sufficient, through the force of the air concussion alone, to bring it down, and they knew they could not chance a close shot from the long-range guns in the fort.

Though the machines now evoluted at greater height, the powerful glasses enabled the observers to plainly distinguish the movements below.

It was quickly manifested that the garrison lookout had become aware of the aërial visitation, and that they did not approve of the color of the hovering aircraft.

A couple of smokeballs ascended and burst in the center of a cloudrack far to the right of the machine. Renos broke his record for silence with a shrill cackle.

"Save your powder, you numbskulls," he shouted for his own satisfaction.

Roque seemed oblivious of the gunplay below. As the biplane described great circles over the fort, he kept his glasses steadily aimed at a point in the enclosure over which the flag was floating.

The men who emerged from the officers' quarters all wore the French uniform.

Roque had evidently cleared up a disturbing point in his mind as he muttered something about a "fool story," and "I might have known there was nothing to it."

Having satisfied himself that it was still an independent little war at this remote point from the main field of operations, and that he had been misled by some advices previously received, the chief observer passed the word to his pilot to back-track, at the same time giving signal to the companion biplane.

As the machines swung around for the return flight, and drew closer together, Renos gave a megaphone yell through a hollow formed by his hands:

"Speed for your lives, they're on the wing!"

Above the gentle slopes on the west, leading to the summit of the mountain ranges, aircraft had arisen, looking, at a distance, like black dragonflies.

At the same moment, the invading biplanes also had a reminder to hurry from the fortress they were leaving behind.

A shell burst seemingly quite close to the machine Henri was driving, and the craft dipped far to one side.

Billy's heart beat up to his throat when he saw the break in the flight.

But his was an exulting cry when the momentarily stricken flyer righted, and bored ahead.

"Glory be!" hoarsely rejoiced the boy from Bangor, when his chum again drew to the upper level.

Seventy miles an hour was the clip of the fleeing biplanes, and no less speedy the onrush of the aircraft from the slopes.

"Steady, and a little to the right," Renos instructed Henri.

The observer was resting the rifle barrel on the rigging, awaiting a broadside target.

Sping! One of the attacking aviators was first with his rifle, and the bullet nicked the armored side of the German craft. Sput! Henri heard an angry exclamation behind him, and shifted an eye long enough to see that Renos was nursing a bloody wrist on his knee.

"How hard are you hit?" was the anxious question of the young pilot.

"Nothing to kill," replied the observer, as he used his uninjured fingers and his teeth in knotting a handkerchief above the wound so as to compress the severed artery.

With the utmost calm he then deliberately used his left hand in rifle aiming, and sent a bullet into the nearest hostile machine.

Whether the shot crippled the pilot of the leading pursuer, or whether it was the menace of the heavy howitzers on the German frontier, which was now of short approach—the French flyers suddenly ceased to be aggressive, and with a parting salute of rifle practice, turned back toward their mountain station, while the German machines dashed across the line of safety.

Upon landing Billy indulged in a sort of war dance around his chum.

"Thought you were gone that time, sure, Buddy," he cried, "and it was simply great the way you pulled out of the hole."

"I guess I was stunned for a minute, as though somebody had hit me with a hammer," explained Henri, "but when I found the controls were still working, it was a bracer, I tell you. And if there isn't a cool head" (nodding toward Renos, who was inspecting his wounded wrist) "I never saw one. He stretched his arms over me ready to take hold if I failed to rally, and did it as a matter of course. Not a tremble about him, either."

"What do you think of the No. 3's now, boys?" queried Roque, when he had dispatched Renos in search of a surgeon.

"They're dandies, all right," promptly agreed the happy pilots.

"They will do to hunt trouble with, anyhow," laughed the secret agent, who was immensely pleased with the flying achievements of the day.

Roque, pluming himself with the idea that, though he did not hold Ardelle when he had that

artful dodger under his thumb, he had at least
chased his rival out of the empire; and, having
also eased his mind as to the report of a new element in the Alsace campaign, he was impatient in
his preparation for departure. Master of detail
though he was, the big moves only appealed to him.

A great battle was raging at Soissons, on the
Aisne river, in France, and Roque had in mind
an aërial journey north, and quick flight across
the border to the scene of the fierce artillery duel,
following the line of march of the mighty force under General von Kluck.

The crippled Renos was replaced in the observer's perch by an aviator known as Schneider, a
very daredevil, and who was at first inclined to
doubt that the boy with whom he was paired had
sufficient skill and courage to pilot a military biplane in an active war zone. Henri very quickly
convinced the doubter that he was very much older
than he looked when it came to the fine points of
aëroplaning, and, too, that when there was an
emergency demand for "sand" the youngster had
plenty to spare. Schneider had additional assurance of capacity when he was advised that both
of the lads carried Roque's indorsement of efficiency.

It was a bitter struggle that the Aëroplane Scouts
were to witness at Soissons, and six days of it had
already passed. The earth was still dropping on

many graves of the German fallen, and yet, sprawling in attitudes along the heights, in the deep-cut gorges of the plateau, and across the flat valley bed were French infantrymen in their far-to-be-seen red-and-blue uniforms, swarthy-faced Turcos, colonials, Alpine riflemen, and bearded territorials.

At staff headquarters, in the first officer that passed near them the boys recognized a familiar figure, no other than Colonel Muller, whom they had first met in far-away Texas, U. S. A., on the day of the record flight, and again in the hangar camp at Hamburg.

Billy impulsively stepped forward. "How do you do, Colonel?"

The officer instantly turned in his stride to inspect the speaker. "Hello, Boy Aviator," was his hearty greeting. "How under the sun did you ever get here?"

"Same old way," said Billy, "the airline, of course."

"And here's the other one," the colonel reaching for Henri's shoulder.

"By the way," continued the big soldier, "this must be a field day for flyers. Here, Hume, come and see what the wind brought in."

The officer addressed moved at quickstep in response to this invitation. It was the aviation lieutenant from Hamburg. He grinned from ear to ear when he laid eyes on his former charges.

"Can't lose you if I try," he exclaimed. "Have you enlisted with us?"

"No," laughed Billy, "we're still driving cars for the good merchant from your town," with the backward point of the thumb at Roque, who was engaged in close confab with a group of staff members near by.

"Did you blow in with Schneider, too?" asked the lieutenant. "I just want to say that you will bore a hole in a stone wall sometime if you train with that fellow. Nature didn't give him red hair without reason."

"Now that you are here," broke in the colonel, "you must not be allowed to get out of practice. I expect that one of you will have to give me a ride along the front before long. I have lost three horses this week."

"We'll do our best to oblige you, colonel," volunteered Billy.

It was no merry jest, that ride Billy gave the colonel!

At the time, the French retained a foothold north of the river at only one point—St. Paul—where the bridge from Soissons crosses, and this by a perilous margin, since the bridgehead was completely commanded by German artillery on the heights.

The battlefield entire covered a front of about seven miles, the center and eastern flank a high, level plateau rising steeply a couple of hundred feet from the valley of the Aisne. On the western side a deep valley ran northward, bounded on either side by turnpikes. An airman taking the big curve of the river would not be considered a good risk for a well-regulated insurance company.

But it could be done—and Billy Barry furnished the proof.

When the next day broke a bloody conflict was raging between the two turnpikes, the French infantry attack on German trenches preceded by a terrible artillery bombardment, a storm of shell and shrapnel.

Colonel Muller beckoned Billy to his side. They stood together on the heights from which the French had been expelled only the day before.

"My boy," was the brisk address of the officer, making a field-glass survey of the smoke-crowned landscape, "I am going down the line, and I am to do the distance in an aëroplane. Is it you or Schneider who will do the driving?"

"You gave me the first call yesterday," reminded Billy.

"That was my intent, and it still holds. I was only seeking to learn if you were of the same mind since that powder mill let loose down there."

"I well know the odor of it," stoutly maintained Billy, "and it doesn't weaken my knees."

The young aviator, accepting the matter as settled, hastened toward staff headquarters. "Mr. Roque," he excitedly called, "Colonel Muller wants to try one of the No. 3's this morning, and I'm to pilot."

The secret agent lifted his eyebrows as though surprised, but he really was not. The arrangement had already been made.

"Say, Buddy, this is rough that we can't both go; and suppose something should happen to you?" Henri had just realized that something was up, in which his chum was vitally concerned.

"Don't you worry, pard," consoled Billy, "it is only a little spin of a few miles, and we'll be back in no time."

"Wish it was me," sighed Schneider, for this firebrand guessed that it would be a red-hot journey.

As the biplane swept into the breeze current, trending to the river, which then was running brimful, and in many places overflowing its banks between the two armies, Colonel Muller advised Billy to keep the machine climbing for the time being, as a terrific fusillade was in progress in the distance of the next two miles, the shells hurtling through the air like lighted express trains. In the three steep-sided ravines that deeply notched the plateau on the east French troopers swarmed like bees, and at this cover the big German guns were blindly banging.

"We can't see much, Colonel, at two thousand feet," complained Billy.

"You would see nothing at all if we ran into one of those fragments of shells," coolly suggested the officer, "but never mind, you will do some diving in a few minutes."

Billy got the signal to dip at the juncture of the turnpikes, and to hold a level and lower course along the line of battle, marked here by infantry fighting between the seemingly crawling columns far below.

"Down!"

The colonel's order was peremptory, and Billy forthwith volplaned toward the earth.

CHAPTER IX.

THE LUMINOUS KITE.

THE biplane had hardly scudded its length on the turnpike, when the colonel leaped from the machine, his sudden appearance greeted by salvos, both of cheers and an extra round of rifle discharge.

Billy sat like a statue in the machine, facing a reserve force of grim, gray-garbed veterans standing at attention.

The front rank soldiers eyed the boy curiously, no doubt wondering that one of his years should be serving in the capacity of a full-fledged military aviator on a mission so supremely perilous.

Billy could not understand what Colonel Muller was saying to the commanding officer of this regiment, but he could see the effects rippling through the serried lines, a stiffening of attitude, a closer grip of rifle stock and squaring of shoulders.

The column, solid and compact, the German practice of close formation, moved with clockwork precision down the field to back the general charge against the living wall that barred the way.

"Charge! Charge!" The cry from a thousand throats.

The forces mixed in a struggling, swaying mass, with indescribable noises, the clashing of steel and the squealing of horses, for cavalry had joined the fray.

Billy jumped out of the machine into the dusty road, the sole spectator there of the conflict that raged but a half mile distant.

Colonel Muller had taken to horse and was riding furiously to rally incoming reinforcements for the gray column.

A rattle cut into the sound ruck—the machine guns of the Germans had turned loose, and men were mowed down like ripened corn.

But fainter now in Billy's ears grew the roar of violent contention, alternate advance and retreat serving to shift the tide of battle further northward, and finally stemmed by the final demonstration of the day at Soissons bridge.

Barring the occasional wild gallop of a riderless horse down the road, the young aviator saw no signs of life about him, and he was too far away to hear the groans of the wounded on the sodden field now enfolded by the gathering gloom of evening.

"I wonder if the colonel has forgotten that his carriage is waiting," thought Billy, trying a bit of mental cheer to relieve the strain of his trying position.

The colonel, however, had not lost his memory

along with his hat, for even then a foam-flecked horse was bringing him back to the driver of his aërial chariot. Mud-bespattered from head to foot, he sent a hearty hail ahead of the pounding hoofs of his weary mount.

"Ahoy, my stranded mariner: is supper ready?"

That reminded Billy of a decided vacancy under his belt, but the glad sight of the colonel was the best tonic for a drooping spirit.

"We will wheel this airship out of the way for a spell and have a bite to eat in the trenches."

Concealing the biplane behind a clump of bushes the colonel gave Billy a hand-up, and the horse cantered away with its double burden in the direction of the slopes.

It was about 7:30 when the colonel and Billy climbed over the slippery slopes to the line of reserve trenches, lowered themselves into one of these holes in the ground, and it was evident that the occupants knew how to convert a ditch into a home.

This trench had a head cover formed of crossbeams, overlaid with branches and earth—a sure protection against shrapnel. There was a long bench of telegraph poles, little cupboards for cartridges and kit, and ramps for reclining chairs or couches, and drains to carry off the rain.

"Come into our parlor, colonel," invited one of the soldiers, leading the way into a subterranean

chamber, which was warmed by a fire in an old per-
forated petroleum tin.

"It is wonderful what ingenuity and labor can
accomplish out of the most unpromising material,"
observed the colonel.

"Made in Germany, colonel," laughed one of the
veterans, "no matter where you put them."

From the business end of the trench a hot meal
was speedily produced for the visitors, adding another touch of surprise for Billy.

"Well, my lad, we must report to the general,"
announced the colonel, who had politely denied the
petition of the trench veterans that he try one of
their couches for the night.

"You don't mind an air trip in the dark, do you?"
inquired the colonel.

"Not a bit," assured Billy, "I've made many a
one."

It was quite pitch black when the colonel and
Billy rode back across the plain, but the horse was
sure-footed, and the way was fitfully lighted by
the occasional upshoot of rockets that left a long
green stream of stars, revealing the now silent battlefield and its dreadful record of uncounted dead.

While Billy flourished an electric torch in giving
the biplane a careful look over, the colonel bestowed
a playful slap on the flank of the faithful horse,
which sent the animal trotting up the road.

"He knows his number and troop as well as I

do, and will go as straight as a die to the feed trough," asserted the colonel.

"Are you ready, boy?"

"Trim as a ship, colonel."

With a flare on the compass, rising high, Billy held the nose of the biplane in the direction of the heights that centered headquarters.

Small red sparks glowed in the trenches below, and the upper darkness was ever and anon split by signal rockets and leaping flames of light from countless campfires.

Billy, with the aid of the small searchlight in the bow of the biplane, found safe landing, also insuring a sight of the colors to the sentries, who might otherwise be tempted to take a pot shot at the winged, midnight visitor.

Henri was the first to hear the whirr of the incoming aircraft, for which he had for hours held an open ear.

"Here you are at last!" he exclaimed, making an open-arm break for his flying partner. "You haven't lost an eye, or a leg, or anything, have you?" he anxiously inquired.

"Sound as an Uncle Sam dollar, old boy," assured Billy. "But you just bet I'm sleepy."

"I believe even Roque was uneasy about you," said Henri, as he insisted on giving Billy's blanket a snug tug.

That the secret agent proposed to reserve the

services of the young aviators to himself thereafter and during their stay in this locality was made manifest when he told them the next day to make ready for a quick departure in the biplanes. As usual, he furnished no advance particulars.

It appeared that Schneider was also to figure in the expedition in a capacity indicated by his employment of oiling and polishing a service rifle of the 16-shot brand, and the display of a pair of long-barreled revolvers stuck in his belt.

"He looks like an arsenal on parade," commented Billy when the red-haired flyer, in war-like array, passed on the way to conference with Roque.

"There is no peaceful intent about that get-up," admitted Henri. "And let me make another prediction," he continued, still proud of his last previous success as a prophet, "this isn't going to be any pink tea or garden party to which we're going."

"What a head you have," said Billy, beaming with mock admiration.

There was a decided lull in the fighting this day —the ninth since the continuous combat had been commenced, as the soldiers of the two armies were apparently resting on their arms. Some fresh planning, no doubt, was in progress.

The boys wandered around the camp, restlessly anticipating the expected summons from Roque. The latter, however, had not picked daylight in which to operate, for it was long past nightfall

when Schneider sought and advised the boys that
the starting time had arrived.

The moon was working full time when the biplanes set their course, following the turnpike toward La Fere.

Above a farm, which had practically been razed,
and on the edge of a ruined district, both Roque
and Schneider signaled the pilots to lower the flight,
and the biplanes circled groundward, landing near a
row of stunted willow trees. They showed no
lights, and with the motors silenced lay hidden behind a huge pile of débris, close to a wrecked dwelling, so close that the full moon shining through
the shattered roof gave the aviators a dim vision
of hopeless confusion, cooking pots and children's
toys, broken clocks and tables, knives, forks and
books strewn on the floor, beds and everything
awry.

Billy and Henri had as yet no inkling of the purpose of this mysterious proceeding in which they
were engaged. Their companions did not seem to
be in a hurry, either, to enlighten them. Roque
and Schneider appeared intent in upward gaze, perhaps hoping that the moon and a dense bank of
clouds forming near would soon come together.
As a matter of fact, a total eclipse of the great
orb above did follow, with the effect of the sudden
blowing out of the one lamp in an otherwise dark
room.

Curious to relate, it was not long until the moon was replaced in the now black canopy by a small but quite silvery brilliant imitation of the big illuminant.

The diamond-shaped light in the lowering sky flashed this way and that, as if responding to the manipulation of an aërial cable.

Roque was not puzzling about the appearance of the dancing light; it was the message that it conveyed which baffled him, sent, as it were, from within the German lines, and, maybe, of vital concern—aid and comfort to the enemy.

Sentries on the heights had reported night after night of this queer, intermittent flashing in this very place, and when Roque heard of it, he instantly comprehended the meaning.

Some spy within the lines was using a luminous kite to signal information of value to the foe.

This is what had brought the secret agent, an adept in the same kind of game, flying through the night to scotch the play and the player.

Roque and Schneider skirted the ruins, and stumbled over the plowed ground with all the haste that such rough going permitted. The boys, free of any order to stay where they were, cautiously brought the rear. They were mighty curious to see what was going to happen.

Schneider had taken the electric torch from under the pilot's seat in one of the biplanes, and it had occurred to Billy to follow suit. This precaution served to save the party an ugly tumble or two into forbidding ditches.

The still-hunters had just emerged into a road with a wonderful avenue of trees. The kite telegrapher's hidden nest was near at hand. The position of the kite itself indicated that.

A streak of moonlight breaking through a cloud-rift revealed Roque and Schneider kneeling in the road, and there was a glint of a leveled rifle barrel.

The boys backed up against a tree, expecting momentarily to hear the whip-like crack of the gun. But instead came the bark of a dog—one shrill yelp, then silence again.

The luminous kite, unleashed, followed the moon into the clouds. Roque and Schneider dashed forward, but for nothing else than to use the electric torch in locating a half-loaf of bread, some cheese crumbs and a ball of cord.

The sentry dog had saved its master!

"Nothing to be gained in chasing that fox tonight," growled Roque. "He's deep in the brush before this."

"I'd like to have got a pop at the dog, at least," complained Schneider, patting the stock of his rifle.

The boys having no desire to be the victims of any mistake of identity, marched forward, Billy waving the electric torch, and calling to Roque:

"It's us."

The passwords were unnecessary, for Roque knew all the time the boys were trailing him, but was restrained from objecting by fear of some word reaching the ear of the man they were stalking.

"You gadabouts," he admonished, "you should have been guarding the biplanes instead of prowling around in the dark like this."

The tone of the reprimand, however, was not one of great severity. The boys had disobeyed no order, for none had been given.

"As soon as day breaks," said Roque, as they plodded wearily down the road, "we will continue the hunt in the machines, though I doubt very much whether it will amount to more than a waste of time."

"If I see a man with a dog underneath us, just bring me within rifle shot, young man, and I will show you something fancy in the way of gunning."

Henri, whom Schneider was addressing, mentally resolved that he would be in no haste to perform as suggested.

Conditions, however, were reversed long before this test could be made. Indeed, the reversal, with the dawn, was at hand. The hunters were the hunted.

The thud of iron-shod hoofs, the clank of sabers —a troop of cavalry charging through the wooded avenue—four madly racing footmen in the furrowed field.

Full two hundred yards between them and the biplanes!

CHAPTER X.

THE CARRIER PIGEONS.

Billy and Henri, with much less weight to carry than their stalwart fellow fugitives, and much spryer as sprinters, easily led in the race to the flying machines.

Schneider stopped more than once in his tracks to fire from the hip at the pursuing cavalrymen, but he failed to score a hit until the leader of the troopers had almost ridden him down. One of the long-barreled revolvers emptied the saddle of the rearing charger. Schneider had thrown his rifle away at the last moment, finding his pistol more effective in close quarters.

By this time, the boys, assisted by Roque, who was doing some shooting himself, until all of the cartridges in the revolvers he carried were exploded, had pushed and dragged the biplanes into the road, and ready for the getaway.

Schneider, with a yell, hurled the empty revolvers in the direction of the next comer, then bounded across the first ditch in his way, jammed a shoulder against the now humming machine in which Henri was seated, to give it starting impetus, and at the same instant leaped within the machine.

Both machines were off in a jiffy, and when the cavalrymen in force galloped to the spot, their carbines fell short of range. That they had been chasing airmen was something of a surprise for if they had not been so sure of a capture, the troopers would probably have pumped lead much earlier in the chase.

"Guess he didn't get his man for keeps," remarked Billy to Roque, as a side turn of the aircraft enabled him to look down on the field, where a dismounted rider was getting a helping hand up from a comrade.

"Schneider gave him something to remember, anyhow," grimly replied Roque.

In the other machine the red-topped and red-tempered aviator in the observer's seat was deeply deploring, in no uncertain terms, the loss of a crack-a-jack rifle and two up-to-date revolvers, borrowed for the occasion.

"Hume may toss earth when I tell him his pet irons are gone, but it was a shindy for quick action, and no saving grace."

Schneider evidently intended to tell the aviation lieutenant about the fight before he mentioned the missing weapons.

The next flight planned by Roque was one of long distance—starting twenty-four hours later, and leaving France.

"Good-bye, my young friends, and good luck to

you; if you ever see Colonel McCready again tell him 'here's looking at him.' "

These were the parting words of Colonel Muller, accompanied by a warm hand-grip.

When the flying party finally reached Strassburg, the big German city of the Alsace-Lorraine region, it was a glad day of halting.

They had floated in over a country literally shot to pieces by the concentrated fire of the French and German guns—that is, in French Lorraine—and in the distance viewed the great fortress of Metz. To the aviators it appeared as though the land hereabouts had been devastated by a gigantic earthquake, which had shaken down all the towns and villages into a mass of shapeless, smoke-blackened ruins.

The boys wondered that they did not see more soldiers in the open, and Henri expressed this wonder to his companion in the biplane.

"Oh, but the woods are full of them," assured Schneider, pointing to the small columns of smoke rising here and there from the snow-clad forests.

True it was that these same woods contained thousands and thousands of armed warriors, ever on the lookout, who were gazing across the frontier at the other woods, which concealed countless thousands of soldiers of the Kaiser.

In Strassburg, Roque was again in touch with the invisible strands of the far-spreading web he maintained. Among his first advices was the most disturbing one that Ardelle had returned and had been making some ten-strikes within the borders of the empire.

The boys shrewdly guessed that something of the sort had happened from the renewal of the German agent's habit of charging almost every sort of disaster to the secret work of his French rival.

Roque realized, as one of the profession, what an important factor is the under-cover man who works within the enemy's lines in the service of his country. And with a keen blade like Ardelle, big things were possible, as past performances indicated.

But even Henri, as a self-claimed prophet, had no idea that the man he knew as Anglin would bob up in Strassburg, though the city was as likely a point as any in the war zone for secret service activity.

When Billy jokingly asked his chum if he had any predictions to fit this occasion, Henri admitted that his second-sight "was off the job."

It soon developed that the secret service experts of both sides were matching wits in this quarter. Reported in Roque's calendar of the week was the giving away by one of his workers in hostile territory of a French attack on the Germans during a fog, with the result that the intended surprise resulted in a rout, and the assailing force mowed down almost to a man. The mute testimony was in a low-lying valley out in the Lorraine field—700 graves in a space 200 yards wide and about 50 broad.

Then a counter-move, wherein the French had advices from some source unknown of the coming flight of a Zeppelin out of the Black Forest, and three French aëroplanes were ready to charge at the big dirigible, which, after a continuous exchange of fire lasting forty minutes, made narrow escape to the north, just when the lighter craft had succeeded in getting above it for a finishing stroke.

As it came about, and in a queer way, too, the boys were the first to blunder upon a cunning ruse being resorted to by a smooth worker in getting away information under the very nose of the astute Roque.

Billy and Henri, indulging their liking for high places, and having a little leisure to look around, found a favorite perch in one of the famous towers of Strassburg. They were interested, as airmen, in watching the daily flying exhibit of the pigeons 'round about.

"Have you noticed, Henri, the streak of feathers every once in a while that don't stop to associate with this housekeeping bunch? I've seen two of these birds already this morning; they act just like an aëroplane, circle about, and then break away like a bullet. There's one now. Look!"

Henri followed the aim of Billy's finger, and, sure enough, a long-tailed flyer was cutting the air like greased lightning in a straight line west, without the slightest notice of the many of its kind pluming themselves on neighboring towers and housetops.

"They make long visits," commented Billy; "I've watched, but never see any of these air hustlers come back."

"That's funny," observed Henri, "let's borrow a glass this afternoon and find out, if we can, where they start from. Why, this is good sport; we'll be wearing badges next as pigeon detectives."

The boys had small notion then that they were butting into a real business proposition, but one that did not advertise!

They were just curious to find out from where came the busy birds that would not take time to visit with their brothers and sisters.

The most that the tower observers could discover, even with the field glasses, borrowed without leave from Roque's traveling outfit, was that the next bird comer took its bearings over a red-roofed building, rising out of a circle of tall trees, a full mile to the east.

Had it so happened that Roque was in a social mood, and the boys making him a confidant of their bird study diversion, there would, without doubt, have been no delay in striking at the heart of the problem—and everything else under that red roof.

Carrier pigeons were not beneath the notice of the big man with the delicate touch!

But Roque was not inclined at the time to indulge in fireside fancies. He was hooked up to a procession of events that needed constant attention, and as it was all ground work for the present, he had no use for aviators.

So he missed the first bang at the very musserup of his plans whom he was, day and night, seeking to locate.

"We'll amble out that way to-morrow and learn how to break pigeons of the loafing habit."

Billy had once had a loft full of pouters in Bangor, that, he claimed, ate their breakfast in bed!

"We'll shake Schneider and start early."

Schneider had been detailed by Roque to keep an eye on the boys, but Henri felt sure that this firebrand would not be interested in pigeons, save in a potpie, so he suggested the "shaking" process.

Trained in the sense of location by their aviation experience, the boys proceeded without difficulty to the sparsely settled neighborhood of the red-roof, which they found to be in the center of a neglected garden, overgrown with weeds.

"Don't see any pigeon loft yet?"

Having been a fancier himself, Billy knew how the birds were housed.

"You might also say that you don'c see any pigeons," added Henri. "We've surely run by the station."

"Not on a little excursion like this," maintained Billy. "This is no ghost story."

With the words he led the way up the long gravel walk extending from the rusty iron gate to the front of the house.

"What will we tell them?" he asked, reaching for the brass knocker on the dingy door of the dwelling.

"How will it do to say we are from the gas office?"

"A fool answer fits a fool's errand," agreed Billy as he gave the knocker a sounding rap.

The pounding awakened no sign of life.

"Come on, Billy," urged Henri, "let's go. It's all a crazy move, anyhow, and it was just because we were idle that we ever thought of it."

"I'm going to try the back door," insisted Billy, "and then we'll quit."

There they got a response, probably after an advance inspection. The door was partly opened by a bent, palsy-shaken old man, who in quavering, high-pitched voice inquired their business. The question was in French, and Henri responded:

"We just came out to look at your pigeons, and" —the age fell from the figure in the doorway in the twinkling of an eye, two long arms shot out, and in steely grip the astonished visitors were jerked inside, the door closing with a slam behind them.

"What's the matter with you?" gasped Billy, whose collar had been given a tight twist by quick-grasping, sinewy fingers.

Another violent wrench of the neck-joint was the rude form of answer. Billy's fighting blood took fire, and he launched a kick at his tormentor which sent the latter spinning, doubled-up, clear across the entrance hall.

The jarred one, recovering his breath, leaped like a panther at the Bangor boy, but Henri gave him the tripping foot, and he measured his length on the dusty floor.

The boys were making a break for the door, when a new figure blocked the way, suddenly emerging from a room nearby—a resolute fellow, with a cold, gray stare, backing up a steadily leveled revolver.

"Been stirring up the monkeys, have you, Fred?"

The fallen man raised himself on his elbow and made the air blue for a moment with his wrathful expressions.

"I'll fix you, you whelps," glaring at the sturdy youngsters who had bested him.

"Stow the threats, Fred," advised the cool-head,

who had restored the pistol to his hip-pocket when he sized up the invaders as unarmed.

"What the devil brought you here?"

The newcomer put a snap in the question, but with no change of icy eye.

"What devil sent them here, you'd better ask?"

This suggestion from the battered Fred, who had again regained his feet.

"That will all come out under pressure," intimated the cool one. "As long as you chose to honor us with a visit," he added with quiet irony, "we must get properly acquainted. Show the young gentlemen into the parlor, Fred."

Billy would have started a debate there and then had he not been, as usual, stumped by the French language, which he only understood by fits and starts. He knew for sure, though, that he was in Queer Street, with this sudden shift from the regulation German talk he had been hearing since landing in the empire. It was up to Henri to set matters straight.

Henri, however, had come to the conclusion that the pigeon story was not popular here, considering its effect on the man who had first met them at the door. So he wore a thinking cap on the way to the "parlor."

This apartment was the only one that had a living look, all the others, noted in the passing, cheerless and empty. It was a "sky parlor," being reached by narrow stairway, only a garret between it and the roof.

An old table, rickety chairs, portable cots and a rusty oil stove were in evidence. There was a wide fireplace with no fire in it. It occurred to Henri that the present occupants of the house did not approve of smoking chimneys.

To get a line on what might be expected, he mildly inquired, with a pale smile:

"Now that we are here, for what are we here?"

He was certain that he himself could not win a prize with the correct answer.

The cold-eyed man could not restrain a short laugh in his throat.

"You are the fellow on the witness stand," he said, "but we must wait for the prosecuting attorney to help us along."

In the waiting time the boys could hear through an open trap-door above them the fluttering and cooing of a score or more slate-colored doves, and it had just dawned upon Billy that there was some particular use for the sheets of oiled tissue and skeins of pack-thread that littered the table.

CHAPTER XI.

UNDER THE RED ROOF.

THERE were no additions to the party in the "sky parlor" until after candlelight. The man called Fred was half-asleep on one of the cots, when suddenly aroused by repeated knocking below. He made stealthy descent, listened at the entrance for a moment, and apparently satisfied with the signal conveyed in the rapping outside, cautiously unbarred and opened the door. The person admitted did not come empty handed, for when he stepped from the stair-landing into the upper room he, and likewise Fred, were carrying market-baskets of goodly size.

"Hello, Gervais," was the hearty greeting he gave to the cool one, the latter engaged, with a well-thumbed deck of cards, in a game of solitaire.

"Hello yourself," returned the gamester, dropping the cards, and coming forward to relieve the newcomer of the market basket.

Billy and Henri were seated in the shadow, beyond the range of the candle rays, and at the time escaped notice. Both had started, however, at the first sound of the new voice.

From a side view the make-up was that of a typical huckster of these parts, fur cap, with ear lappets, corduroy greatcoat and cowhide boots. Between cap and collar bunched a heavy growth of iron-gray whiskers.

The boys did not realize that their instinctive move, occasioned by a certain tone in the voice, had not been amiss until the speaker had turned full face.

Even the luxuriant whiskers could not wholly hide the Anglin smile!

Much to the astonishment of Gervais and Fred, and infinitely more to the surprise of the imitation huckster, the boys at a single bound jointly invaded the circle of light and grasped the elbows of their one-time Calais acquaintance.

"What sort of a hold-up is this?" cried Anglin, in startled recognition; "is it raining harumscarum aviators in Strassburg? By the great horn spoon, it's enough to make me believe I've got 'em to see you under this roof."

"I'll bet you knew that we blew in with Roque," proposed Billy, "for you have a way of seeing seven ways for Sunday."

"You win, laddy-buck, on the first statement, but I'm still up a stump on the proposition of how you got into this house."

"We were loafing," put in Henri, "started out on

a pigeon hunt and got the drag when we mentioned it at your back door."

"Pigeon hunt?" Anglin wore a puzzled look.

Henri made quick explanation of the whole affair.

"Ha! I see," exclaimed Anglin. "By the way, you did not happen to mention your tower observations to anyone else, did you?"

This last query had a dead-earnest ring, with a rising note of anxiety.

"Not on your life," assured Henri; "in the first place, the big chief had no time to bother with us; we had no inducement to talk to anybody else, and, all in all, who'd have cared about the bird business, anyhow?"

"Well, it seems there was one fellow who did."

Billy indicated Fred, who was unpacking the baskets.

"There are others," laughed Anglin, much relieved by the boys' statement. Fur cap, wig and false whiskers were tossed onto the mantelpiece, and the huckster was no more.

The baskets had produced a plentiful supply of ham, cold chicken, and the like, and not one of the party could be charged with lack of appetite.

In the glow of good-fellowship, Fred told Billy he was sorry that he had given him so rough a reception.

"Honors are easy, old top," was Billy's jovial acceptance of the apology, "and I am glad now that we did not break any of your ribs when we banged you around."

"Say, Mr. Anglin, I am afraid, after all, that we may bring down trouble on your head. I just know that Roque will be in a great stew when he finds we are gone and will fairly comb the town to locate us."

The idea had begun to trouble Henri to the extent of spoiling the pleasure of this reunion and indoor picnic.

"I have thought of this," admitted Anglin, "but the danger of discovery is ever the same, and I don't believe this will either hurry or lessen it. Besides, we are prepared, or, rather, had the way prepared for us, to make a run on the slightest warning."

This restored to Henri happier thoughts, though he still held belief that Anglin might have been safer if Roque had no special inducement to immediately lead a searching party throughout the city.

That is just what happened, and it proved not an overly-difficult task for the keen tracker to trace the boys to at least the vicinity of the place where they were hidden.

The men under the red roof were soon made aware of the lurking danger by the tooting of an automobile horn in the avenue bordering the grounds north of the house.

It was a telegraph code set in shrill notes, and it was apparent that Gervais, in alert listening attitude, had comprehended the message, even as the motor-car sounded the final blast in its swift passage out of sight and hearing.

The cool one, in most deliberate way, drawled the words: "Look out."

As effective as if a whole dictionary had been pumped through the window by Anglin's scouts.

The chief calmly resumed the disguise of wig and whiskers, while Fred blew out half-a-dozen candles with little waste of breath. With one tallow dip still alight, and shaded by hand, the doorman then mounted the ladder leading to the garret, thereby causing up there great commotion in the pigeon roost.

When Fred reappeared at the foot of the ladder, it could be dimly seen, he wore a broad grin and a wreath of cobwebs.

"When that flock arrives, empty-footed, old Winkelman will swear like a pirate."

Fred had turned every carrier bird but one loose in the night. The exception was fluttering in his hand, blinking its beady eyes at the glimmer of the lone candle.

Anglin had seated himself at the table and was writing a few words on a scrap of parchment, completing which he deftly attached the tiny roll to the pink leg of the feathered envoy.

Fred lifted the window a few inches and released the bird.

With the utmost care every bit of paper, every inch of thread was picked up and stowed away in the pockets of the three men preparing to vacate.

Billy and Henri were busily figuring in their minds just how they were going to come out of the scrape, when the creak of a shutter, under prying force, was heard on the lower floor.

"They're here at last," muttered Gervais, dropping a hand to his hip, on the revolver side.

Anglin laid a finger on his lips, enjoining silence, and tiptoed down the stairway, the others following in shadowy procession.

On the first floor the leader paused. The attempt to force the firmly hooked shutter had ceased, and no new form of attack was for the moment in evidence. Anglin had removed his cowhide boots, and, with velvet tread, then advanced the entire length of the long hall, motioning those behind him to remain where they were.

He was back again in less than five minutes, and whispered:

"The house, I believe, is completely surrounded. They are waiting for daylight, I suppose, to cinch some sure thing, the nature of which they are not quite certain. If Roque is along and thought I was inside, axes would have been working before this."

"They will find a lot here at daylight," chuckled Fred—"a lot of dust."

The party silently made their way through a side passage to what appeared to have been intended as the dining and cooking domain. Gervais had assumed the duties of guide, and he showed thorough acquaintance with the premises by first producing a dark lantern from a cupboard, and then moving directly to the black mouth of a steeply inclined flight of stone steps descending far below the level.

The spacious cellar was divided into sections by partitions of solid brick. But it was at the center of the foundation wall on the west where Gervais halted.

"Give me a leg up."

Fred gave his comrade the required lift, and Gervais secured a hand-grip on a big drain pipe that curved into the wall. He gave the pipe a strong-arm-twist, and the bull's-eye shine of the lantern revealed an aperture in the masonry, into which the climber squirmed.

Hardly had his feet disappeared, when he had turned about with his head out of the hole in the wall and a hand down to help the next comer to scale the space between the floor and the dislocated pipe.

Billy was given the hoist and crawled over the prostrate Gervais into the narrow passage above:

Henri quickly followed, then Anglin, and finally Fred, who lent aid in pulling the pipe back to its moorings.

" 'Snug as a bug in a rug,' " quoted Billy, who was really enjoying this method of getting out of a tight place, even though getting into another.

However, the rounded and cemented passage did not squeeze enough to be uncomfortable, and there was steady draught of fresh air coming from somewhere further ahead.

"The good man from whom you leased this property six months ago hardly counted this as one of the improvements you agreed to make," remarked Anglin as they started to wriggle through the drain.

Gervais laughed. "I didn't do anything to the pipe but what had to be done, and 'a stitch in time saves nine.' "

"It is likely to save three that I know of," grunted Fred.

"You can always count on Gervais to think for the future."

The man so complimented by his chief said nothing, saving his energy for the vigorous use of hands and knees necessary to make progress in the smooth channel.

The journey on all fours ended at a heavy grating, through which faint daylight was peeping. Through the barred opening the outlook was into a deep ravine, with a small stream coursing at the bottom, and a dense growth of small timber and bushes rising to the level on all sides.

Directly opposite the entrance of the drain, in a small clearing on the high ground across the gully, the broad windows of a stone cottage reflected the glare of the slowly rising sun.

"There is nothing else to do, my friends, but to lay low until brother Roque completes the scouring of this section. We are well on the way but not yet out of the woods, as the saying is."

This was the view of the chief, and his views were seldom questioned.

It was a rather gloomy prospect, this crouching wait in quarters so confined, but the secret service men counted nothing a hardship, and the boys had to possess themselves in patience.

The capacious pockets of the huckster's greatcoat, with which Anglin had not parted, despite its weight, in the long crawl, contained a supply of food, taken from the baskets before starting.

From the avenue that lay between the ravine and the grounds about the house which they had recently quitted, the cramped company in the drain could hear the rumble of traffic, and once they heard voices in close proximity to their hiding place.

"Giving them something to puzzle about, eh, Gervais?"

"Rather a fuddle for them, chief," agreed the

cool one, "and the best of it all, they don't know whom they're after, unless it be these youngsters."

"Oh, I propose that the boys shall be found in due time, but the balance of us will keep dodging to the best of our ability."

"Some ability, too, believe me, boss," was Billy's contribution.

"Well, I believe we can hold our own," complacently observed Fred.

With the wearing of the long day, the prospect of liberation eased the trial of the later hours. As night fell apace, the first greeting to it was the glow of a lamp in one of the windows of the stone cottage.

Gervais moved close to the grating, and fixed intent gaze upon this illumination. In the course of a half-hour his vigilance was rewarded by a sight that he evidently anticipated. Somebody was repeatedly crossing and recrossing the patch of light, now and then deliberately standing in front of the lamp. That "somebody" was making dots and dashes as plain as day to the trained vision of the receiving expert.

"The coast is clear," he announced.

A little pressure and the bars were down.

Out into the night crept the weary five, with the luxurious experience of once more standing erect and having a good stretch.

Having replaced the grating in the drain entrance

to a nicety, Gervais led the way down the steep slope of the ravine to the creek, which Billy and Henri attempted to drink dry, so great was their thirst.

"Now is a time when the best of friends must part," said Anglin. "I have been thinking it over, and the suggestion is that you, my young friends, must be relieved of any suspicion of willingly associating with suspicious characters. Gervais, Fred and I have our mission clearly mapped, the cause we serve is supreme, and the safeguarding I propose is of mutual benefit. With you boys here we can have no open acquaintance, and of us, as we are, you must claim no memory. To be brief, you have been detained by rough characters at the other end of town, and you will be there discovered at the roadside in the morning bound and gagged and stripped of all your possessions."

"I am afraid we are mighty poor picking," joked Billy, "but it is all right to give us the truss up, as we brought this shake-up to your door."

"That is neither here nor there now," consoled Anglin; "we must mend the situation as best we can."

And so it came about, at a point remote from the red roof, a passing policeman picked up two much hunted boys who were decidedly the worse for wear.

CHAPTER XII.

THROUGH FIRE AND FOG.

"You're a pretty pair, I must say."

True it was, the boys were not fixed for any dress parade when they first faced Roque, immediately after their delivery to the secret agent by the police authorities. The crawl through the drain pipe and the additional effort to give them the appearance of real victims of violent treatment, had served to convert the usually natty and trim youngsters into a couple of quite disreputable looking characters.

It is quite likely that Roque would there and then have put the returned wanderers through the "third degree" of questioning had it not been for a fortunate and welcome interruption in the shape of a messenger, who could not be denied, and who, it proved, brought tidings that wholly changed the line of thought of the stern chief.

"Take these chimney-sweeps to the tub and the clothesline," he gruffly ordered, and Schneider, half concealing a broad grin, accepted the service with celerity.

"You ought to have heard the boss when he

found that you had not reported at quarters last night," said the red-topped aviator, when the trio were out of Roque's hearing. "He took the wind out of my sails, I tell you, and I am not considered slow in the cussing business.

"Where were you, anyhow?"

"In the hands of brigands, of course," gravely advised Billy, with a wink at Henri.

Schneider was so possessed with the prospect of some new and exciting move by Roque, indicated by the manner of the chief upon receipt of the message a few minutes before, that he did not burden the boys by forcing evasive explanations of their mysterious absence.

"If Roque had half a suspicion that we had been in company with his pet enemy, the prince of slyboots," confided Henri, when the chums were alone, "our joint name would be Dennis."

"Gee! If that fellow hadn't bumped in just at the right time, I think we both could have claimed the title of Ananias!"

Billy was a poor hand as a dodger of truth, and much relieved to escape the witness stand in this instance.

The kind of danger with which the boys best loved to toy was again speedily coming to them— the peril of aëroplaning.

Schneider brought the order to report forthwith at the aërodrome.

At the aërodrome an immense Zeppelin airship, as long as an ocean liner, had just been inflated. Roque was engaged in conversation with the captain of the great dirigible when Schneider and his young companions reached the grounds. The pilot of the huge craft and his assistants had already taken their places in the front gondola, the foremost end of which had been screened for their protection, and it was evident that sailing time was near. When the master mariner had exchanged a parting word with the secret agent he entered his room in the central cabin of the Zeppelin, which was in telephonic communication with the front and rear gondolas and other parts of the ship. In the meantime, Schneider had instructed the boys to give the No. 3's an inspection to see if the attendant helpers had properly prepared the machines for a long journey.

The young aviators then surmised that they were to travel as convoys of the monarch of the air, which even then was majestically rising.

Roque hastened to the machine in which Billy was already seated and waved a signal to the waiting Henri in the other biplane, containing also the redoubtable Schneider.

The swift flyers easily overcame the slight lead of the big ship, though it was making 40 knots, and took up the guiding positions. The flight was directly away from Lorraine and historic Strassburg.

"I wonder if our huckster friend is in the crowd back there?" was a mental question with Billy.

It was many a day before the young air pilot had a chance to again meet Anglin.

When this journey ended it was in territory remote from that of any former experience of the Aëroplane Scouts—a new battle landscape. It had snowed, and the drab, brown plain of Poland had turned to glistening white. The biplanes floated in a tarnished silver sky, which, pressing down, seemed hardly higher than a gray ceiling. The aviators landed on the clay bank of the winding yellow river, the Bzura, within 400 paces of the German trenches. Gun answered gun across the golden stream, shell on shell spattered into the soft earth, and rifles rattled unceasingly.

Schneider sniffed the powder smoke like a seasoned warhorse. "It's the life!" he exclaimed.

"And the death," added Roque.

He knew that men lay bleeding and broken on the banks of this yellow streak in the white picture.

"You're just right, boss," murmured Billy, nodding his hooded head, "the war map looks all red to me."

Roque, as usual, wherever he went or wherever he was, seemed to carry an Aladdin magic carpet on which to sail, for in the next flight of the bi-

planes a few miles distant he found a bright spot
in this winter scene of rack and ruin—a clean,
white lodgekeeper's kitchen, where a canary sang,
and where the aërial wayfarers rested and were fed.

"I'll show you even better," he said, "when we
break into Warsaw."

The chief also had a particular crow to pick with
the defenders of the Polish capital. One of his
men, for some time operating with the Russians,
had been detected, and the end of a story of brilliant secret service achievement was marked by a
little mound of earth in a Warsaw stable yard.

But for the present there were busy days ahead
for the aviators in reconnoitering the Russian lines.

Most of the aërial work here was over a plain,
flat as a floor. Black dots here and there marked
isolated houses, and the Kalish road was bordered
by a line of leafless trees with smooth trunks, which
reminded the young pilots of a rank of grenadiers.

"What's that bunch over there?" queried Billy,
nodding toward a group of horsemen, shrouded in
long caftans, wearing lambskin caps shaped like a
cornucopia, and bearing lances.

"They are Cossacks," replied Roque, from the
observer's perch, "the strange fighters who never
surrender."

Billy had later an opportunity for closer view of
these reckless riders in the service of the Czar.

The flyers could see that the road below was

this day crowded with the carts of refugees, trailing in endless procession, on the top of each vehicle the members of the family, the average one man to five women. The boys noted that there were not so many children here as they had seen among the homeless wanderers in Belgium. The same problem was here, however—what are they going to do?

"There they go again," cried Henri, referring to renewed outbreak from the long gray noses sticking out over the top of a brown gun emplacement —belching cones of death, and shooting red flare into the gray-white atmosphere. Then another noise out of the winter-worn copse of trees—pop, pop, pop, the notes of rifle fire, all raising a queer mist over the plain. With all this racketing no soldier could be seen at the point of fire.

If trouble was contagious, the biplane Henri was driving suddenly caught some of it; something went wrong with the motors, and it was a case of get down quick in the long slide, in which performance the young pilot excelled. He landed safely enough, but without choice of place.

The machine was stranded in Sochaezev, a city of the dead. Pale faces were still peering from some of the doors and windows, though almost every roof had been battered in, leaving only the stringers, reminding one of skeletons.

Billy had instantly volplaned in pursuit of the disabled biplane of his partner, and the two experts, assisted by Schneider, were speedily at the work of repair.

Roque impatiently moved about among the ruins, acting as a sentinel, and occasionally turning to the laboring aviators with muttered insistence for haste.

"Hist!"

With the chief's sibilant warning the boys softly laid down the tools and motor parts they were handling, and stood at attention. Schneider drew a revolver from his belt.

Roque, in crouching attitude, held an ear close to the frozen earth surface, and the others took example.

"There's a cavalry troop headed this way," hoarsely whispered Schneider. The pounding of many hoofs, growing louder and louder, was a sound apparent to each listener.

Then as a new diversion, out in the open field to the right of the road, down which the horsemen were galloping, rang out the rapid blows of pikes and spades on the ice-covered soil.

"They're throwing up kneeling trenches."

Schneider had a true ear for war moves.

The grating noise of the closing of a gun breech preceded a tense moment.

By the shifting of sound it was impressed upon the listeners that the oncoming cavalry had left the road and had swung into the plain on the left.

"We'll be between two fires in a minute or so."

This from Roque, as he rejoined his companions standing by the aëroplanes.

"Give us a precious ten minutes and we need not care," volunteered Henri, who had discovered the defect in the machinery which had brought them down.

"Get at it, then," urged Roque.

The boys did "get at it" so vigorously that they raised a perspiration, despite the frigid air.

"It's all right now," triumphantly announced Billy, hastily repacking the tools.

That they had been spared the time required to meet the emergency was due to the fact that the cavalrymen had diverted their course so as to make a sudden frontal charge on the artillerymen from the cover of the ruins.

"Now for a move backward," ordered Roque in low tone; "even though the gunners to the right may wear the gray we would have no show for recognition if we bounced up like a flock of partridges."

So the aviation party cautiously wheeled the biplanes in the deserted street as far as they could from the supposed line of the coming clash.

None too soon were they out of range, for with savage yells the Cossacks rode full-tilt from cover at the German guns and gunners in the shallow trenches.

Amidst the roar of desperate conflict the biplanes whizzed away like great arrows.

"Some speedy tinkering we did in that ghost town, Mr. Roque?"

"Nothing slow," assented Roque, leaning forward to give Billy a pat on the back.

"Where away now?" asked the pilot.

"Back to the lodge for the night," directed the chief.

No such comfort for the boys in the next flight. They were booked for a journey to Przemysl, the vast underground fortress of Galicia, about which the Russian right end was then snapping like the tip of a whip around a sapling, and later surrounded on all sides by the Muscovite forces.

While viewing the first back-wash of the Austrian forces from the high tide of Russian invasion, the aviators had hurtled through a maelstrom of noise. The yells and shoutings of wagon drivers, the rattling of thousands of wheels over stony roads, the clatter of horses' feet made an indescribable tumult, and to this were added the sounds of infantry fighting.

Roque had reliable advices during one of the stops in the flight that the fortress defenders were still holding their own, and no Russian charge had as yet crossed the barbed wire mazes that circled the city.

Never since the memorable race at Friedrichshaven had the No. 3 type of biplane attained such velocity as in the finish of this forced run to the Galician stronghold, the final dash over the black-plowed farms through a wet fog and under fire of a Russian battery posted in the hills.

"I feel like I had been hauled through the lower regions by a nightmare," complained Billy, as he later sat with Roque, Schneider and his chum in the Steiber Coffee house.

"I will say," confessed Schneider, "that I never hit the wind so hard before in my flying experience. My eyes must look like two burned holes in a blanket."

"I might say, Schneider," remarked Roque, "that if it had not been for that timely fog you would have hit the ground harder than you ever did before. Those gunners on the hill could not have missed us if given fair sight."

"It has just occurred to me that they came pretty close, anyhow."

"They sure did, Buddy," laughed Billy, following this assertion by his chum. "I almost collided with a shell that sounded like a dozen factory whistles. By the way, Mr. Roque," he continued, "it looks like you were tied up here for some time to come. I don't see any way out of it."

"Do not lose any sleep over that problem, young man; if we got in we can get out. You ought to

know by this time that there is always a hole in
the air that cannot be blocked."

"You bet he's right," exclaimed Schneider, slapping his knee for emphasis.

"Hustle for bed, all of you, and stay there until
you are called."

With this the chief faced the fire and lighted one
of his big, black cigars. He had some thinking
to do.

The boys were awakened the next morning by
gunfire.

"Oh, lawsy," sleepily murmured Billy, "is there
another battle started already?"

Schneider at the first report had gone on his bare
feet to the nearest window.

"Nix, fellows," he cried, after short observation, "they're not shooting at men this time, it's
wild geese they're popping at."

The besieged garrison was adding to its store of
eatables by bringing down wildfowl, which flew in
abundance over the town.

"Let me in on that."

Henri owned the idea that he was something
of a full hand as a Nimrod.

A voice in the doorway: "You will be 'let in' on
bigger game than that."

Roque smiled at the youthful enthusiast, and
added:

"There is a man's size job for a half-sized man waiting until you shake the sleep out of your system."

"Get up, you snowbirds, and sing for your salt."

CHAPTER XIII.

CAPTURED BY COSSACKS.

"COLONEL, permit me to present a likely pair of air travelers who are never satisfied with the ground space they occupy."

Billy and Henri tipped their caps to six-feet-three of superb manhood, in Austrian uniform of dark blue.

Roque made the introduction, and the boys felt quite sure that this ceremony only completed advance notice of the character of service they were capable of rendering.

The officer, measuring the young aviators with a keen gray eye, nodded approbation.

"They will admirably fit in the carrying service," he remarked to Roque; "they are jockey weight, which is a good point for the assignment."

Billy assumed from the manner, if not the language used, that Henri and himself had successfully passed inspection.

It appeared that airmen here were persons of some importance, as affording the only connecting link with the outside world.

Almost every day, the boys were advised, an

aëroplane went to Galician headquarters, on the outward flight carrying only letters and postcards, but on the return trip bringing tinned meats and hand grenades for the soldiers.

The big biplane piloted by Billy and Henri dwarfed anything else in the way of air machines shown in the fortress.

Other aviators, viewing the No. 3's, cheerfully conceded that they were certainly built to be winners.

These experts, however, as usual with their kind just getting acquainted with our boys, were inclined to be doubtful of the capacity of the youngsters to rank with themselves as drivers of aircraft.

It was up to time—a little time—to convince them of their error of judgment.

The crack driver of the Przemysl air squadron, Stanislaws, which name Billy promptly shortened to "Stanny," was the earliest convert to the new belief when he went as observer with the boy from Bangor on the latter's first foraging detail.

Lack of knowledge of the country prevented the chums from working together at this period.

"He will show me the way, but just hazard a little guess that I'll have a little show of my own on the way."

Billy buzzed this in the ear of the grinning Schneider, when the order to get away was received.

Henri, with the comfort that his turn was coming, stoutly backed the belief that his partner intended to exceed the speed limit as a lesson to the doubters.

" 'Stanny' will have a new kink in his whiskers before he gets back," was the expression, to be exact, used by Henri on this evening.

The great bird machine, soaring like an albatross in the northern sky, soon vanished from the view of the watchers in the fortifications.

"He's six horses and a wagon with a dog under it," Stanislaws earnestly advised the officers at army headquarters, pointing at Billy, who was reducing heat in the propeller by liberal use of the oil can.

"Stanny" had already made good with the American boy, not so much by his frank expression of admiration for the youngster's handling of the military biplane as for the reason that the Austrian talked plain United States when they were alone. Billy was dead-set against the trial of eternally groping for the meaning of foreign phrases.

"Do you know why we aviators are running a freight line just now?" queried this new friend.

Billy acknowledged that he had not the least idea on that subject. "Why?"

"Filimonoff."

"Who in the dickens is Filimonoff?"

"He is the greatest of all Cossacks," explained the senior airman, "and the very devil on two sticks.

Near Przemysl, not long ago, he held up one of our convoys and captured 200 wagons of grain and coal. He strikes where least expected, plays the peasant to perfection and secretly gets a lot of information that does not belong to him. It would be worth a lot to a fellow who dulled the spurs of this cock of the walk."

"Ah hum," thought Billy, "I can pretty near guess now what brought Roque to this neck of the woods."

So long was the enforced wait at headquarters this day that it was not until after nightfall that the biplane set out on its return voyage to the fortress.

A strong air current from the north, with a decided snap to it, forced the aviators out of fixed course, but despite the biting blast Stanislaws was yet able to advise the pilot as to the general direction to be pursued.

They saw ahead of them a red glow and the uplift of a spreading fountain of sparks. It was a house burning to the ground, probably fired by a Russian shell.

The blaze revealed a familiar landmark to the biplane observer. "Keep her nose to the left," he advised the pilot.

Billy, who figured the speed fully 70 miles to the hour, had the machine under perfect control, and it instantly responded to every shift of the steering lever. With the ordered slight turn it was scarce ten minutes before the biplane hovered over the vast, shadowy mass of the fortress below. The powerful propeller stopped, and the winged racer stood still against the black dome of the midnight sky. Now the forward plane dipped as the throbbing of the motor again was heard, and the bird machine plunged down at an angle of 45 degrees, settling in the plaza within the silvery ring formed by its own searchlight.

"The work of an artist," proclaimed Stanislaws to the aviators in the night watch.

"Carrying some weight, too," added the soldier who superintended the removal of the cargo.

Billy had a bedtime story for Henri about Filimonoff.

It having been determined to regularly use both biplanes in the carrying service, the detail at last put the boys together in the same machine, with Stanislaws and Schneider manning the other.

"None of your self-made adventures," Roque admonished, when he had informed Billy and Henri of the arrangement.

The young aviators were, in duty bound, compelled to mumble some sort of assurance that they would stick closely to the task set for them.

That they failed to keep the agreement proved, strange to say, the fault of Schneider, the very man charged to keep an eye on them.

It was the third aërial expedition of the week, and following the same route, without mishap, had no longer the charm of novelty to Billy and Henri, and, it may be stated, the easy sailing had begun, also, to pall on the high-strung warrior with the sorrel hair, now sitting as observer behind the Austrian pilot.

At army headquarters, Stanislaws was giving his entire time and attention to checking up the needs of the garrison, and figuring closely on the capacity of the biplanes to carry all that he deemed absolutely necessary to take back to the fortress on this particular return journey.

The balance of the crew—the trio who were getting weary of the uneventful freight business—had nothing special to do but wait.

"No use of sitting still and twiddling our thumbs; I don't see any harm in looking around a bit."

Schneider's suggestion appealed to his companions, and they had no trouble in securing the loan of a pony each from the large number of these hardy specimens of horseflesh browsing around the camp.

They were advised by a good-natured member of the commissary department not to venture too far beyond the line of patrols, and Stanislaws gave them to understand that he expected to be ready to start within the next three hours.

"We'll be here on time all right, Stanny," called

Billy, clucking his pony into a smart canter, following the lead of his similarly mounted friends.

The one who was left behind had no reckoning then that he need not have hurried in his packing.

The roads traversed by the riders were deep in slush and mud because of a thaw, but the fresh ponies reveled in the going, and it was not long before a tempting range of harder ground extended the gallop further afield.

"Say, boys," suddenly remarked Schneider, rising in the stirrups for a survey of their whereabouts, "I think we have gone about far enough, and must take the back-track immediately."

"Wait a moment," urged Henri, "there's a man waving to us over there."

Schneider, looking in the direction indicated by the boy at his side, saw it was a peasant who was making the friendly motions to attract their attention.

"What's the word, my friend?"

The peasant spread out his hands in gesture of cordial yet humble greeting. "My house is near" (pointing eastward over the plain). "It is yours."

"The sun is yet high, let's go over and see the house of his nobs," gayly proposed Billy.

The native shrugged his shoulders, and wore a puzzled look at the words in a tongue evidently foreign to him.

Henri supplied the information in German, it

being the language in which the invitation had been extended to them.

"I think he could understand even better if we were talking Russ, but still, as he made a fair stagger in German, we will have to let it go at that. We can see him home, as he says it is near, and then strike out for headquarters."

Prodding his shaggy steed with his heavy boot-heels, the stranger showed the path to his guests, the party speedily reaching a small but solidly built farmhouse on the bank of a small river.

Schneider, with soldierly precaution, transferred the heavy service revolver he carried in his belt to a convenient pocket under the cape of his overcoat.

Perhaps the husky fighter felt it was not much of an exhibit of courage to set a gun at hand when he found that no other human than this old farmer with a crook in his back seemed to inhabit the premises.

"I was as dry as a fish," asserted Billy, eagerly accepting a drink of cold water from a stone mug proffered by their host. There were other thirsty ones in the party, for the mug was emptied several times in the passing.

Just about that time Schneider lost all interest in water. Happening to glance out of a window facing to the north, his eye caught a sunflash on a lance-head, and now and again other sparkling tips.

The revolver he now appreciated was in the right place.

But of what avail, after all, was one pistol against a band of reckless and wily Cossacks, if such were under those nine-foot lances?

Billy and Henri were unarmed.

The peasant was up with a jump when Schneider proclaimed his discovery of impending peril.

"Hide! Hide!"

With the words of alarm he tugged at an iron ring in the center of the heavily-planked floor.

It was considerable of a lift, this weighty trap-door, but the old man developed a surprising degree of activity and strength, and quickly presented the way to a cellar by means of a ladder, the length of which indicated considerable depth.

"Not for me," strenuously objected Schneider; "they will never catch us like rats in a trap."

"Quick! Quick!" pleaded the peasant.

Billy, at the window, excitedly announced:

"They're the real thing; I can tell by their caps and caftans. The Cossacks are here!"

Schneider was as cool as a cucumber—that was the way the near prospect of a death struggle always affected him. He was hot-headed only when given the smaller provocations.

"Bar that door!"

The boys hastened to obey that crisp command.

The old peasant attempted to leave the house before the entrance barrier was secured and fastened.

"Halt!"

An unwavering line of steel barrel, and the menace of the voice behind it, checked stockstill this attempt to escape.

Fully a dozen of the rough riders of the north had dismounted in the farm enclosure, and advanced upon the house, some with lances and others carrying curved swords without guards.

"Get away from the windows," hissed Schneider, himself backing against the wall. "You too," savagely addressing the peasant, who in the past few moments continued to show remarkable recovery from the infirmity of bent shoulders and halting step. The man nervously fingered the folds of his rusty green tunic as he obeyed the fiercely given command, and as he stood nearest to Billy the latter was inclined to keep at least the corner of his eye peeled on the suspect. It was well for Schneider that the boy was watchful, for when the supposed farmer stealthily lowered his hand it grasped the bone haft of a dagger.

The Cossacks outside vigorously pounded the door with lance butt and sword hilt, and receiving no response to their peremptory summons, set powerful shoulders to work. But they could not budge or even shake the solid barrier.

Then at the window appeared a bearded face of

ferocious type, surmounted by high-crowned lamb-skin cap.

Schneider slowly raised his revolver.

The transformed peasant, noting the action, crouched like a panther for a spring, which he made the same instant. But the murderous intent was baffled and the leap fell short.

Billy Barry's foot was purposely in the way, and the would-be dagger wielder hit the floor with a crash. Startled by the tumble, Schneider's trigger-finger caused the waste of one revolver shot, and spoiled further attempt to deceive by silence.

In the moment of excitement no thought had been given by the defenders to the rear of the house, and before Schneider could even turn on his heel, a half-dozen lance points threatened him, front and back.

The fallen peasant was on his feet in a flash, and it was a mighty ugly look that he fixed on Billy.

"You will go to the cellar now, because I say it, and will come out again if I will it."

The sign of leadership was on the man, for none of the strange soldiery about him ventured to speak even a word in his presence.

Schneider, disarmed and no longer resisting, was hustled into the dark hole in the floor, and the boys were forcibly assisted in the same gloomy descent.

The heavy trap was closed with a bang, and sealed by the crossing of a clanking chain.

CHAPTER XIV.

A WONDERFUL RESCUE.

"Blamed if I oughtn't to be treated for the simples."

Schneider was, indeed, a dejected figure at the foot of the long ladder in this inky well, the only point of light being a porthole sort of window, set high in one of the four stone walls.

"We're all of the same name as chumps," echoed Billy.

The situation certainly had serious aspect to the prisoners. While they had considerable confidence in the trailing ability of Roque, here was a case with about every chance in the world against successful tracing.

An isolated farmhouse, far from the beaten track, not even in present line of military operations, and confinement practically in a granite tomb, from which no wail of distress could possibly be heard outside.

What fate the Cossacks had fixed for them was merely a matter of dreadful surmise.

"Slow starvation," was Henri's unhappy guess.

"Penned up in this den until we go mad," was the blood-chilling view of Schneider.

"Say, you fellows give me the creeps."

Billy wanted his troubles one at a time.

The next one was all too near.

While feeling his way around the rocky walls, Schneider settled in his tracks as though he had been shot.

"Don't you hear water splashing?" For confirmation he stared blankly at the boys who had not as yet strayed away from the ladder.

"Are you starting your madhouse already?" demanded Billy.

"But there is water running near," insisted Schneider. "Come over here, if you don't believe it."

As if to humor their friend, the boys joined him.

Sure enough, the lapping sound was plainly audible at this point.

Further ahead in the dim recesses of the cellar the sound was of dripping, a steady patter like rain.

"Maybe they have pulled a sluice between here and the river," suggested Henri.

"The fiends," muttered Schneider.

"Gee!" exclaimed Billy, starting back from a forward step or two, "the floor is filling!"

Stealing along, inch by inch, the water spread throughout the cellar.

The prisoners retreated to the foot of the ladder and sought perches on the rungs. In case of full flood they could stave off drowning for a time by climbing higher. It was the only way.

"It's a pretty tight place we're in, old man, but not for the first time, and, mind you, we have always pulled out somehow."

Billy was ever ready to pass a cheering word to his chum when cheering words were most needed.

Schneider's nerve was again in the ascendant, he having sufficiently abused his lack of horse sense in being so easily led into such a trap.

"If I had hold of a good steel pike for a bit of an hour, there is nothing like a few planks that would keep us down here."

"Yes, or a couple of axes, or a stick of dynamite, or an electric torch, and so forth," bantered Billy.

While Schneider and Billy were word sparring to keep up their spirits, Henri noticed that the water on the cellar floor had pooled in the sunken spots, indicating that the pressure from without, for the time being, had largely subsided.

"No need for life belts yet," he cried, "the river isn't going to come through."

"And, thanks to that blessed streak of light," Billy pointing to the bull's-eye window, "we're able to see that you are right. So much for a starter."

"We'll beat you yet."

Schneider shook his fist at some invisible foe on the other side of the ceiling.

When, however, the first flush of encouragement at the fading of the flood had dimmed, it seemed a small matter about which to rejoice. The situation appeared as hopeless as before to the imprisoned aviators. With the coming of night the one diamond in the sable setting vanished—no ray of light to slightly relieve a condition now of absolute blindness.

"Oh, for one more glorious chance to meet those dastards in the open," groaned Schneider, who again was overwhelmed with keen regret that he had surrendered at all in the first place. But then he had no idea of such a dungeon as this, and, too, he had feared to provoke instant death for his young comrades.

In the coming dismal hours the troubled trio, deserting their ladder perches, stretched their aching bones upon the slimy floor, and passed the night in uneasy slumber.

Henri was the first to awaken, and as a morning exercise essayed to reach the little window by working hand and toe as a means of scaling the rough surface of the wall. As he clung for a fleeting moment to a protruding stone his chief discovery through the aperture was that outside it was raining in torrents.

Perhaps not much satisfaction in return for sadly torn fingernails and considerable waste of already waning energy, yet it was some assurance that they were not intended victims of a drowning plot of man's conception.

"It's not the river that is feeding this drip," announced the climber to his companions in misery, "it's raining like fury and the water coming in here is the gutter fall through these rocks."

"A bally lot of moisture," growled Schneider, splashing ankle-deep across the cellar to inspect a swinging shelf which had just caught his eye.

He reached up, and presently turned, holding at arm's length a mouldy sailcloth bag.

"Hidden treasure," whooped Billy. "Bring it nearer the light, Schneider."

The treasure proved to be meal of some sort in a fair state of preservation. A tasting test demonstrated that here was something that would at least dull the gnawing pains of hunger, when mixed with water, of which latter there was more than a plenty.

"We might make a fire out of the shelf," suggested Henri, "and turn this stuff into hot cakes. I've got a few matches in my pocket."

"I see a picture of the fire you could make down here," exclaimed Billy. "But what's the matter with trying it out on the trap door? Burn our way out."

The speaker had taken on an air of excitement at the prospect.

Alas! The matches in Henri's possession had been carried on his sleeping side, the side all night in contact with the slimy floor.   There was not a strike in one of them.

Schneider, inveterate smoker that he was, remembered that his pipe, tobacco and match-case were all in the pocket of his great coat, of which the Cossacks had divested him after capture.

So in silence the unfortunate three mouthed the soaked meal, bitterly disappointed that they could not realize upon Billy's brilliant idea.

From bad to worse, they did realize, and soon, upon a much less desirable development. The rain had no stop this time to reduce the water flow into the cellar. In restoring the meal sack to the shelf for safekeeping, Schneider's long boots were wetted to the knees, and there was nothing to do but mount the ladder, and stay there.

To save a fall when napping, the prisoners lengthened their belts and buckled themselves each to a rung above the one upon which he sat.

"While you were wishing awhile ago, Schneider, why didn't you wish for a boat?"

"You'd joke on the way to the scaffold, young man," said the subdued firebrand, fixing a reproachful look on Billy.

"Never say die," retorted the irrepressible youth.

Another wearing night, and in Schneider's next trip for the meal bag his hip boots were none too long in the matter of preventing his taking on a cargo of water.

But this third day of desperate contemplation was destined to be marked by an incident which resulted in the lifting of the weight of gloom—and the herald of light and liberation from an apparently hopeless imprisonment was four-footed.

A few lines now in backward trend, to tell about the ambulance dogs, as many as a thousand, renowned for their excellent service for the Germans in both the eastern and western theaters of war. Each of the sanitary companies has attached to it four of these dogs, the German shepherd breed, marvelously trained and fitted for work on the battlefield, commanding everywhere eloquent tribute for their remarkable performances in finding the wounded and their acute scent on any trail.

Stanislaws had long completed his packing of the biplanes, and many a time and oft had impatiently paced Commissary Square, as many times going to the military road upon which he had last seen his aviation comrades riding joyously away. " 'Stanny' was in a stew," as Billy would have put it, and he was not averse to letting anyone about him know it.

When night came word was passed from patrol to patrol, and back again, and no definite report of the missing aviators.

An observer was secured from among the young officers in the camp, and Stanislaws himself piloted one of the biplanes on the return journey to the fortress.

Roque was immediately advised of the mysterious disappearance of his three followers, and promptly indulged in some very emphatic comments not appropriate for parlor use.

"You must fly again in an hour," he raged, "and I'll be with you."

Stanislaws, though weary and nerve-strained through the exertions of the long flight just concluded and by the weight of anxiety, would not listen to the offer of brother aviators to relieve him of the added exertion of repeating such a journey without rest.

"I'm going back with him," he stoutly maintained —and he did.

At headquarters Roque took advantage of the first glimpse of daylight to institute work of inquiry, in which practice he was conceded to be without equal. But to no avail. The furthest outpost had seen the riders pass, and, fully satisfied with their credentials, had paid no further attention to their movements.

Somewhere out on the boundless plain, alive or dead, were the three so earnestly and expertly sought for.

"It's a hard nut to crack," Roque stated to a group of officers, "but I have opened just such hulls before, and I am not ready yet to plead inefficiency."

"Perhaps they have fallen into the hands of the enemy," said one of the officers.

"I can hardly believe that an old campaigner like Schneider would run into the lines of the foe with his eyes open. If suddenly attacked by lurking prowlers, I'll warrant we'll find some sign, for I know the man too well to believe he would be taken without a struggle and somebody biting the dust."

Roque had evidently not figured on Schneider's present handicap in the shape of the boys, forcing discretion ahead of valor.

Then the winning thought flashed into the mind of the secret agent—put the ambulance dogs on the trail!

The reminder was the approach of one of the sanitary officers. The latter, when he was told of the situation, at first presented a doubtful front.

"The heavy rains out there," said he, indicating the plain by a sweeping movement, "have drowned the scent, even if we had a good lead from this point; but," he concluded, noting the disappointment in the face of Roque, "I do not mind making a try for it. Here, Blitz."

The splendid animal bounded to the side of his master, lifting expressive eyes, and indulging in a series of short barks, showing readiness to serve in the best dog language.

Hasten, dog, there is sore need for aid in a dark place of yonder sea of mud!

Schneider, Billy and Henri had not ventured from the ladder since the early move after the meal-bag, which the first named had decided to keep within reach, and save further wading to the shelf. The flood on the floor showed no sign of receding —indeed, the trio had twice been compelled within the hour to climb a little higher to escape the splash at their feet.

Schneider, anything for diversion, pounded on the trapdoor until his knuckles were a bleeding mass, shouting until he was hoarse.

"What's the use?" he dully questioned, settling again into an attitude of sullen indifference.

The boys set up a duet, but with discord so apparent, even to themselves, that they quit the singing attempt as a matter of self-defense.

This noise had hardly ceased, when Schneider poked his head around the ladder support on the side of the light, with a hand hollowed behind his ear.

"Jumping jingo; listen!"

They all heard at once the snuffing of a dog, and with the sight of its black head stuck into the bull's-eye window, Billy dropped into the flood, breast deep, and struck out for the wall, up which he swarmed, regardless of scrape or strain.

He had seen the ambulance dogs in camp, and

knew of the breed and their doings. Holding onto the narrow ledge like grim death with one hand, he used the other and his teeth in tearing out the scarlet lining from his cap, which he twisted around the dog's collar band. Blitz—for Blitz it was— whined his receipt for the red token, backed from the aperture, and padded away like the wind.

Two hours later the trap was lifted, and the exhausted survivors of this desperate adventure were hauled into daylight, joyfully greeted by a goodly company, including Roque, Stanislaws, sanitary officers, pioneers, and last, but not least, Blitz, tugging at the line by which he led the rescue party to the scene of his original discovery.

CHAPTER XV.

DUEL TO THE DEATH.

SCHNEIDER was a very walking furnace, with his burning desire to meet again, on equal footing, any individual of the Cossack band that had thrust him, lamblike, into the stone tomb under the farmhouse, and, particularly, the fake peasant for whose wiles he had so foolishly fallen.

"Give us a biplane hunt for that gang," he importuned Roque, "or I will never get the red out of my eyes. Filimonoff himself might have been in the crowd, for all I know, and you ought to be doing some tall bidding for his headdress. It was just like one of his tricks."

The firebrand felt that he had hit the mark with the last part of his heated argument. Roque would have counted full reward for the chase in the bagging alone of the wily chieftain of the strange horsemen.

He turned to Stanislaws, remarking: "You men for awhile will have to resume the use of your own machines in the carrying service. I have concluded to give Schneider a chance to retrieve his blunder and return a lesson that will stick into savage hides."

"We won't stand in the way for a minute," quickly and earnestly stated the Austrian flyer, "and more power to you, sir. What's more," he added, "we can spare an aëroplane or two, and I know several full-blooded lads who would be mighty willing to join such an excursion."

"Meaning that you are one of the volunteers," rejoined Roque. "How about it, Schneider?"

"It is hitting the nail on the head," heartily approved the brick-top warrior, "Stanislaws, Breckens, Bishoff, and Mendell—there's two crews that would help some."

"What's the matter with us?"

The Aëroplane Scouts had edged into the circle. The idea of a biplane hunt especially appealed to them.

"Sure you're going," proclaimed Schneider, glancing first at Roque for sign of assent, which was given by a nod.

Four military biplanes twelve hours hence lay in readiness to start for the Cossack roundup. The Austrians in the party carried a supply of bombs for emergency work, but the most elaborately armed of all was Schneider, in the rôle of chief challenger. He bristled with revolvers, a shoulder-hung carbine and a heavy cavalry saber.

"If you should have a fall, old fellow," laughed Stanislaws, "it would sound like a barrel of tinware rolling down a mountain."

"Never you mind," said the one-man arsenal, "I have a job of making sieves on hand."

The plan was to hover for a time in the vicinity of the farm where Schneider and the boys had been held up, or, rather, down, and if no sight of the Cossack company, to reconnoiter still further north.

The flyers were given a great send-off by the soldiers at headquarters.

"Just like a balloon ascension at a county fair," observed Billy, as he took his place as pilot in front of Roque.

"Something new here, I see," Henri calling the attention of his aviation companion Schneider, to the fact that Stanislaws had provided telephone helmets for each of the crews, whereby pilot and observer could communicate with one another without yelling their heads off, receivers over the ears and a transmitter close to the mouth.

"This will save my voice for singing," jollied Henri.

Schneider, remembering the vocal effort in the cellar, came back with the expression of hope that the telephone invention would not serve to that extent.

"Oh, but you are a jealous cuss," declared the boy, as he guided the machine upward, in compliance with the signal given to all by Roque.

"We have all the advantage this time," 'phoned Billy to Roque, when the flight was well under way;

"if the outfit below is too heavy for us we can stay out of reach; if we feel that we can lick them, a dive will settle the question—our choice both ways."

For the first few miles all the creeping figures below were of the friendly forces, but with the onrush of the aëroplanes all traces of the camp were obliterated and only a trackless waste presented itself to the view of the lofty travelers.

Directly, Schneider reported to his pilot that the farm enclosure was just ahead, with its yellow ribbon border, which the river wound around it.

The observers on the four biplanes gave the premises a thorough looking over with their glasses, but had no announcement to make of any human movement below.

Separating the machines, each distant from the other several hundred yards, the pilots guided northward, at reduced speed, and within a few hundred feet from the ground.

Some twenty miles forward, the little fleet encountered a snowstorm, and the earth was already covered with a dazzling white carpet.

A range of hills forced a higher flying altitude, and in an atmosphere growing decidedly chilly. The aviators were quickly compelled to close their coats at the throat, and to huddle down in the protecting folds of their service blankets.

On a high level, Roque instructed Billy to make a stop, so that the long sitting airmen might work the cramp out of their joints by a brisk runabout. The snow had little depth on the wind-swept plateau, and landing could be made with smooth certainty.

A spot of blackened surface showed bare through the powdery snow covering, indicating a recent campfire there.

"Trot out the coffee pot," Henri called to Schneider, "here are the makings of a blaze."

The recent heavy rains had filled with water the rocky basins near at hand, and the thin skim of ice now forming thereover was easily broken.

The Austrians elected tea as their special inspiration on the occasion, and the rival fumes soon ascended from the spouts of coffee and teapots.

As the sky above was now clearing, from the elevation the aviators could see the brown and white summits of other hills, divided by valley cuttings, as far as the eye could reach.

Schneider was just about to light his beloved briar pipe, when all of a sudden he dropped the ember he was lifting to the bowl, and pointed toward the high ground edging the opposite side of an intervening gulch to the right of their bivouac.

A solitary horseman had ridden into view, and both rider and steed posed, statue-like, on the verge of the steeply descending slope.

Roque like a flash covered the smouldering fire with a blanket, checking tell-tale spirals of smoke.

Fixing a glass on the equestrian, Stanislaws uttered the one word—"Cossack."

"He's our meat," snapped Schneider.

"It's your first go this time," reluctantly conceded Stanislaws, who was himself aching to draw first blood.

Schneider, taking general consent for granted, gave Henri a nod sidewise, and both moved as quickly as they could on all fours to their biplane. While the boy was getting the motors in play, the fighting observer shifted his carbine from shoulder to knee.

The buzzing of the aëroplane had evidently caught the ear of the wild cavalryman across the gulch, for the horse was rearing, lifted by an unexpected wrench of the bit.

Nothing, however, on four legs or two, would have a ghost of a chance to outdistance a racing aëroplane.

Spur as he would, the horseman was overhauled in the space of three minutes.

The aëroplane, skimming the earth, mixed its scattering of snow particles with those raised by the pounding hoofs of the wildly galloping horse.

So close together were pursuer and pursued, that the Cossack's first lance thrust came within a hairline of reaching the ribs of Schneider, leaning forward in preparation to make a flying leap from the aircraft when it should lessen speed sufficiently to enable him to keep his feet when alighting on the stony soil.

Why the observer did not immediately use carbine or revolver in return for the lance attack, queerly impressed the young pilot ahead, who, naturally, would expect such action on the part of his armed companion, gravely menaced by a wicked weapon too lengthy to be successfully resisted by counter strokes of a saber.

Henri's second thought was that Schneider had been touched in a vital spot by the steel point, and that he, too, would next get into the deal of death. To send the machine aloft was a third thought, following in a flash, but the execution of this purpose was as quickly delayed by a motion indicating a lift of weight behind. Schneider had jumped from the biplane, now wheeling the ground, and within two lengths of a precipice, hitherto unobserved.

The Cossack, on the very brink of this dizzy declivity, had jerked his horse to its haunches, at the same moment when Henri checked further movement of the biplane by a skillful side turn.

"It's you and me for it now," roared Schneider, "and the devil take the quitter!"

Turning in his saddle, the Cossack, desperately at bay, accepted the challenge with ferocious alacrity, backing the fiery animal he bestrode and taking to foot with drawn sword.

Henri saw that it was the same man who in the

guise of a peasant had played them such a scurvy trick—the same, but yet seeming hardly possible, viewing this upstanding, powerful specimen of a hardy, unconquerable race.

Schneider, never forgetting a face, had known the impersonator at the first glance, which added to the incentive of wiping out the score created by the Cossack company at the farmhouse down on the plain.

Noting that his adversary was armed only with sword and dagger, having blunted his lance against the armored side of the biplane, the aviation firebrand discarded his carbine and pistol, tossing them one by one onto the snow carpet. He had the notion of settling this affair in a manner that would completely retrieve certain prestige of which he conceived himself to be the loser.

In the meantime, the balance of the aviation party swooped down upon this level, and leaving their biplanes, advanced to the scene of the impending duel.

"Keep back, all of you," shouted Schneider, the bloodlust gleaming from his eyes; "it is one to one here, and though he put twenty to one against me, I will give him his chance, and take mine."

"Better humor him," suggested Stanislaws in an aside to Roque, "he will never rest easy if he does not get rid of the black mark he has rubbed on his own nose."

"He may get a red mark or two in this combat," grimly observed Roque, "but let them fight it out. Schneider ought to be able to take care of himself."

Billy and Henri followed with fascinated gaze the movements of their champion, who, though he sized up almost half a head shorter than his extremely tall antagonist, was all wire and a swordsman without equal in the estimation of the Heidelberg student body.

The duelists indulged in no time-saving tactics. Schneider rushed his man from the outset, but every rapid lunge of his heavy saber found clashing counter from the curved and guardless steel in the practiced hand of the wily Cossack.

Forward and back, ever fiercely fencing, the sworn foes panted defiance at one another, and each with blasting words renewed efforts to strike a death blow.

"Oh!" Billy had seen blood dripping from Schneider's left sleeve, and leaving a tiny trail of carmine splotches in the trampled snow. In agony of apprehension, the boy again fairly shouted: "Don't let him down you, Schneider; look out for the next!"

Roque gave the excited lad a muttered order to hold his tongue.

"Ha!" This from Stanislaws. A scarlet seam crossed the forehead of the Cossack, and he wavered for a second, as if partially blinded. Only for a second, though, did his sword arm hesitate. Schneider received another wound, this time close to the throat.

"He's done for," tremulously whispered Henri, wondering why the soldier onlookers did not interfere, and eager to make a saving move himself.

Then, as though a whole row of wine glasses had been riven by a knife stroke, the Cossack's blade, cleft near the haft by a biting downward cut of the saber, fell tinkling at his feet.

This was the last flare of Schneider's waning strength, of which, however, the Cossack was apparently unaware. He did not wait to meet an expected heart thrust from the victor.

With a piercing yell, he turned, waved the sword stump about his head, and leaped far out into the void before him.

Schneider, on hand and knee, game, but all in, as the saying is, mournfully shook his head, and faintly murmured: "He would have had another chance to finish."

Stanislaws, something of a surgeon, stanched the blood welling from the wounds of his comrade, applied bandages, and soon had the fallen fighter on his feet.

The Cossack's mount had disappeared, a fact first noticed by the acute Roque. "Mark you," he predicted, "that riderless horse will be sure to stir up a wasps' nest, and somebody here will get stung if we attempt to hold this position. Schneider's punctures are enough for one day."

Roque's prediction was a sure shot, for he had hardly ceased speaking when a score or more of horsemen charged from the cover of a rocky defile and bore down in force upon the aviation party.

"To your places!" thundered Roque.

The pilots of the several aëroplanes were already making ready for hurried flight, and Henri, in addition, had assisted the wounded and weakened Schneider to his seat in their machine.

Breckens, Bishoff and Mendell emptied their carbines and revolvers in the direction of the oncoming lancers, clearing a saddle or two, and swung into the rigging of the waiting biplanes just in time to permit a clean getaway.

Right over the brink of the precipice the start was made—it had to be the quickest way—and a thousand feet of ascent gained without an upturn.

Circling about on high the soldier-observers scattered the horsemen on the plateau with a shower of bombs.

Schneider had had his innings, and returned in full measure all that was owing.

CHAPTER XVI.

DRAWN FROM THE DEPTHS.

"WELL, Mr. Roque, if you did not get Filimonoff this trip, you struck mighty close to him, for I'll warrant the man whom Schneider vanquished was a leader in the Cossack horde."

"And something of a fighter, you might add, Stanislaws," rejoined the secret agent. "But there's another day, and the kingpin and I may yet lock horns."

The aviation party was again at Galician headquarters, and the interesting invalid, Schneider, was already declaring that he was as good as ever.

Roque had a grouch, chafing because of the delay of the Austrian forces in getting through to the relief of Przemysl.

"Just think what might be done if we had enough flying machines, Zeppelins and aëroplanes, to bring over an army corps every week or so." This idea expressed by the ever-enthusiastic Stanislaws.

"You are not talking airship now, Stanny; it's an air castle you have in mind."

This pleasantry on the part of Billy turned the laugh on the Austrian aviator, in which he joined himself.

"There's one thing sure," finally declared Roque, "I know of at least two airships that are soon to sail over the heads of the Russians who are now blocking the way to the fortress."

"I just knew he would be pushing something across before long," said Henri to his chum.

"From the way he looked at us when he spoke, it's safe to believe that we will be somewhere behind the push."

Billy had a hunch that his job was secure whenever Roque had work above ground.

Schneider had heard enough to set him at the task of cleaning and polishing his personal stock of firearms.

The four biplanes returned that very night to the besieged fortress, from which two of the machines were destined to leave in short order on a most important and perilous journey.

Our boys had instructions to give the aircraft a thorough going over, fill the petrol tanks to utmost capacity, and carry all the condensed foodstuff possible.

"Maybe he is figuring on a chance of a lay-up in the mountains," suggested Stanislaws, detailed to assist the younger aviators in the work of preparation.

" 'Maybe' is a good word to use in connection with the moves of the chief, for you can't prove anything by us."

The present was all that counted with the busy lads, hustling to complete their immediate assignment.

"Ready and waiting," they soon announced to the chief, who simply nodded approval, and went on with the work in which he was engaged—studying and making field maps.

Henri put in the spare time afforded with continuous instruction of his chum in the German language, Billy having already acquired, by hard knocks, talking knowledge of French. They were thus occupied one morning, when Schneider appeared, in war-like array, with brief order.

"Buckle up."

Roque found everything in shipshape for the getaway, and smiled at the impatience of Schneider, who had been stamping around the hangars since the first glimpse of daylight.

While the young pilots were drawing to the elbows their fleece-lined gauntlets, the secret agent was earnestly assuring the commander of the garrison of his belief that the way would very soon open for the long-expected relieving force.

"I think I can advise them to good effect if we get through in safety," he said, mounting his perch in the biplane, and giving Billy the word to go.

As the biplanes shot through space, only Roque, the directing power, had knowledge of their destination, though Schneider inferred that the finish would be somewhere in the thick of battle.

This inference was not far amiss, for when the aircraft finally slackened speed, and stood still against the blue vault of heaven, still as the condor floating above his native mountains, the aviators looked down upon a thick forest of bayonets, shown on all sides by the square formation of the Austrian forces, then endeavoring to pierce the Russian front near Lupkow and thus relieve Przemysl.

"We are in the Carpathians," Schneider advised his flying mate.

The fighting in these mountains had then been continuous and intense for weeks, the two armies contending desperately for the ridges, the possession of which would give advantage to the holders. Every concession of a few yards of the rocky slopes had exacted heavy toll of lives.

Behind the Austrian lines at Lupkow the aviators made landing, descending through a sea of smoke, and amid deafening roar of furious conflict.

Roque had hasty conference with the commanding officers, and outlined conditions at the great underground fortress, to save which this day's engagement had been planned.

Schneider and the boys had received orders from their chief to stand by the aëroplanes, and on no account to leave their posts.

"He evidently does not believe there is much of

a show of smashing the Russian barrier to-day," observed the firebrand, who little relished the infliction of standing still in the rear while so much powder was being burned in front.

It was soon apparent, the way the tide of battle was turning, that the rear of the Austrian position would not be such a lonesome place after all. Retreat had begun, and immediately Roque emerged from the ruck.

"This isn't our day," was the news he brought; "get under way or you will get under foot."

It was a stirring scene that spread under the rising biplanes, the massed formation attacks of the Austrians hurled back again and again by the sheer weight of the Russians, pouring men forward in seemingly unending numbers.

"They're thicker than flies in Egypt," growled Schneider, when his soldierly eye perceived that the Austrians could no longer stand the pressure of the numbers arrayed against them, and that the day was lost.

The aviators decided to adopt the manner of the eagle and nest high that night. They found a level on a mountain peak not very far removed from the clouds.

"You could cut the stillness up here with a knife," asserted Billy, and his companions agreed that there was a decided difference between the shell-rent territory from which they had just flown and the awesome silence of this sublime height.

"It might also be mentioned that the cold on this top could be sawed into chunks," put in Henri, taking the precaution of covering the motor tanks with blankets.

Schneider volunteered to skirmish for some material with which to establish a campfire, while the boys busied themselves in opening some of the tins enclosing the food supply.

Roque found consolation in keeping alight a long black cigar.

Presently he concluded to follow in the footsteps of the wood hunter, and hasten the prospect of a cheery blaze by the time night should fall.

With the passing of an hour or more, and no sign of the fuel seekers, Billy and Henri developed an uneasy streak, rendered more acute by the drear surroundings and the oppressive lack of all sound.

"We had better do some scouting; I'll go daffy with this waiting business."

"I'm with you, Billy," joined in Henri, "anything but sitting 'round here doing nothing."

The boys lost no time in picking their way through the rocks in the direction taken by their absent companions.

"Let's give them a shout," suggested Billy, himself acting first on the suggestion.

No answer to the shouters, when they paused at intervals, hoping for the welcome response.

Stumbling along, careless now of bumps and bruises, the lads so often raised their voices to high pitch that they were hoarse from the effort.

Rounding a huge boulder that blocked their path, Billy, who was in the lead, suddenly started back with a cry of alarm, and Henri instinctively threw his arms about the waist of his chum.

Lucky move, this, for the Bangor boy was in the closest kind of way connected with a mass of crumbling earth that swept with a slight rumble into the darksome depths of Uzsok pass.

Henri's strong pull landed both boys on their backs—but on the safe side of the boulder.

"Narrow shave that, old boy," murmured Billy, raising himself on his elbow, and reaching for the hand of his chum, "and it's to you that I owe——"

"No more of that," interrupted Henri, "it's only a rare occasion when you were not doing something for me. I think we can account now for the disappearance of Roque and Schneider. It completely unnerves me, though, to believe that our companions are lost in this abyss."

Billy was on his feet in an instant, alert and resourceful.

"There's a way of finding out whether or not they are down there, and we will never quit searching as long as there's a speck of hope."

Gingerly skirting the boulder, he found solid ground on the higher side, to the right of the treacherous spot on which he had so narrowly escaped a long fall.

Stretched out full length at the verge of the steep descent, Billy peered into the depths, giving vent to several ear-splitting whoops in rapid succession.

A faint halloo finally came back from the dim recesses of the pass.

"Glory be!" cried the strenuous hailer, "there is somebody below—and that somebody is alive!" Through the hollow of his hands Billy shouted words of encouragement to the unseen owner of the voice answering from the bush-grown wall of the chasm.

"It's a clear drop of twenty feet, and smooth as a billiard ball before the growth begins and the rocks shelve out," Billy advised his chum, the latter to the rear and maintaining a firm grip on the ankles of the venturesome prober of the pass mystery.

"Oh, for an hour more of daylight," lamented Billy, as dusk began to envelop the lonely mountain. "Gee! Why didn't I think of it before?" Imbued with his new idea, he quickly swung around, bounced to his feet, hauled Henri up by the wrists, and triumphantly demanded:

"What's the matter with flying around there in the machine?"

"But it's getting too dark now to see anything in that hole," objected Henri.

"Where's your wits, Buddy? What do we carry searchlights for?"

"I sure am a woodenpate," admitted Henri, using a fist to tap his forehead; "let's go to the biplane as fast as our legs will carry us."

The boys raced like mad for camp.

With every light available from both machines set in one of the biplanes, fore and aft, the young aviators sailed through the shadows, got their bearings from the big rock and fearlessly swooped into the lower strata.

The glittering gondola of the air trailed a line of illumination along the rugged face of the chasm wall, but in the first passing, Henri, as observed, gave no signal of discovery.

The insistent hum of the motors prevented the hearing of any hail that might be given from without, and as effectually drowned any call from within the machine.

"Another round, Billy boy," shouted Henri, "a little lower down."

The next circle and come-back brought results, attested by a gleeful hurrah from the observer.

"There's a man on the ledge over there—there's two, by jingo! Round again, pard. Steady now!"

The aëroplane was dangerously near the ledge, a little above it. Henri was standing, one hand

gripping a stay for balance, and in the other grasp-
ing a ball of whipcord. With a sharp turn the pilot
nosed away, the tail lights of the machine gleamed
full for an instant upon the dark figures silhouetted
on the rock face, and in that precious, fleeting instant, with a round arm swing, Henri sent the cord
ball, unwinding as it dropped, straight down upon
the ledge.

"Up!" sang out the maker of the successful
throw, and as the biplane made almost perpendicu-
lar ascent, it tugged, kite like, at a long line of cord,
paid out by one of the men left behind on the rocky
shelf.

Once out of the canyon, the pilot checked his
flight at the first level, and both boys, under the
glare of the searchlight, speedily spliced and knotted
two coils of fine-fibered rope, part of the flying
equipment.

Henri, leaning over the edge, drew the cord connection taut, indicating to the holders below that all
was ready at the top. The boy felt sure that Roque
would understand—for it was Roque he had seen
in the circle of light when the ball was thrown.

Sure enough, the cord was drawn downward,
and the rope followed the cord, with, happily, plenty
to spare for the making of a safe and secure anchor-
age.

"Roque is something of a sailor, as we know, and
he'll come up all right, with a good purchase for his

feet against the wall. As for Schneider, the three of us can hoist him, if necessary."

Billy's advance arrangement went somewhat awry, for it was Schneider's red top showing first in the light over the brink, and Roque was the one hauled, almost a dead weight, to solid ground and safety at the end of the swaying rope, looped under his armpits.

The secret agent's right hand rested in an improvised handkerchief sling, and his face was set in the pallor of pain.

But how strangely gentle had grown the piercing fixity of those hard-speaking eyes when turned upon the rescuers who had dared so much in a feat wonderful to record in aviation annals.

"You might have waited until daylight," he chided, his voice freighted with emotion, "and with less risk to yourselves."

"And the morning found a couple of maniacs cavorting around this wilderness. No, sir, the rest cure wouldn't have been the right prescription for us. Eh, Henri?"

"He's as right as a trivet, Mr. Roque; we took the proper tonic," assured Henri.

"A man's size swallow for all that," was Schneider's amen.

CHAPTER XVII.

A MIGHTY STONE ROLLER.

CAREFUL examination revealed that Roque's injury was not of broken bones, but a severe sprain, due to the twisting suspension from the bush which had checked his fall. Schneider had gone down feet foremost, breaking through the growth until he struck the ledge.

"I didn't expect Mr. Roque so soon," he said, with a face-wide grin, "but I knew him by his legs, and gave him an open-arm reception."

"Until Schneider reached for me," related the secret agent, "I though there was nothing underneath but the bottom of nowhere. It was certainly a curious accident, all in all, the two of us tumbling as we did, stopping in the very same place, and both of us alive to tell it."

"There was mighty near a good third on your peculiar track," interposed Henri, "for Billy had set his heels for that very slide which you two took."

"If it had not been for Henri," asserted Billy, "there is no telling how deep I would have gone."

"And if it had not been for both of you, there was hardly more to look for than a miserable end for Schneider and me. We could have proceeded neither up nor down, for there was nothing to put hand or toe into for many rods either way."

Roque did not propose that the boys should lose any of their dues for gallant achievement by other belief than that two lives had actually depended upon their prowess.

When Schneider intimated that he thought it was time for another attempt to find material for a fire, there were two young rebels emphatically against the proposition.

"We'll move where there is wood in sight," was the joint declaration.

Roque agreed that a change of base was desirable, and a flight from the mountain top was in immediate order.

As the machines descended and followed a lower course, ghastly reminders of the struggle that had recently taken place in and along the pass were easily discernible from the lookout seat of the biplanes —the melting snow on the slopes revealing many bodies of Austrians and Russians.

In a clearing at the edge of a considerable forest the aëroplanes again settled, the observers being first convinced that there was no military occupation, especially hostile, of the wooded tract.

"This beats the mountain roost a mile and a half," declared Billy, the leader in hopping out of the aircraft.

In a big hole in the ground, dug by the impact of a cannon ball, Schneider started a brush fire, and in a few minutes was passing hot coffee around.

"I must say," observed Roque, between bites at a sandwich of corned beef and hardtack, "that I don't seem to be getting anywhere on this trip except into pitfalls. All this is sheer waste of time. I had hoped to see a relief march to Przemysl begun within a day, but here we are tied in a knot, and not a step forward."

"Well," consoled Schneider, "you gave them the route that could be won with the least difficulty."

"But what's the good of that when the opening wedge couldn't be driven?" impatiently queried Roque.

Schneider scratched his head. He had no answer.

"There is one thing sure," exclaimed the secret agent, "and that is, I must be on the move, for this isn't the only fish scorching in the pan."

Billy just then edged into the conversation. He had made an alarming discovery. The petrol supply in the biplane tanks was at low mark. The aviators had expected to replenish long before this, and the disaster at Lupkow had spoiled their last chance.

"Oil nearly out, sir," were the words that brought Roque to his feet like a jumping-jack.

"The devil you say!"

Here was a quandary that completely upset the chief.

"We ought to have filled day before yesterday," explained Billy, "but you know why we didn't."

"The only thing to do that I see," advanced Henri, "is to add the supply of one machine to that of the other, and two of us hunt for the new camp of the Austrians."

"They could fix us all right," assured Schneider, "for there is quite a number of aëroplanes with the force which was driven back."

"It was my intent to get in touch once more with this corps, but it was not my intent to divide this party in the going. It cannot be helped, though, and it may take but a few hours at most. You are sure" (turning to Billy) "that you cannot raise enough power for both motors to go the distance?"

"I fear, sir, that both machines would be stranded in less than an hour; and, with all this uncertainty as to how far we would have to go, there is no telling into what kind of place and under what circumstances we would be compelled to drop. There would be much less odds against the one-machine plan."

"It's up to you to prove it," challenged Roque, "for you and I are going to make the trial."

The transfer of the petrol accomplished, Schneider and Henri were left in sole possession of the camp in the woods, after a last strained look at the departing biplane, a little blot on the sky, finally dissolving in the mist of the mountain top.

"Let's knock about a bit," said Schneider, suiting action to the words by starting up the nearest slope, where the gloomy pines were farther apart than in the dense growth below.

"Ah! Here's where the Russians must have gotten a severe jolt. See here, my young friend"— Schneider pointing at a scattered ground array of discarded rifles, knapsacks, sheepskin coats, and many caisson shells in baskets. "Not so very long ago, either, for you will notice that all this is on the top of the snow and not under it. You can safely wager that here, and at this season, it is not very long between snows."

Here and there were other objects, stiff and stark, that sent a shudder up Henri's spine.

Picking their way still higher to the apex of the ridge, the man and boy had view of a land depression, bowl shaped, almost cleared of snow by exposure to the sun, being free of shade or shadow.

Something on the far side of the bowl, catching a golden ray from above, glittered like a big diamond. Henri called Schneider's attention to the flashing point.

"Worth a walk across," conceded the soldier-aviator, moving that way. Henri, interest aroused, made it a point to outpace his companion.

Drawing nearer, the investigators saw, in half-sitting posture, back against a blanket roll, a soldier —in dark-blue uniform, Austrian infantry—marked by emblems of rank, including a sparkling decoration on the breast.

A silver flask lay close by, alongside of sword and belt.

Schneider dropped to his knees, seized one of the nerveless hands of the officer, and fingered the pulse of the lifted wrist. The old campaigner had noted that the blood curdle in a tunic fold was yet unfrozen.

"Hand me that flask."

Henri quickly complied with his comrade's request, first unscrewing the metal top. Schneider tenderly moved the head of the officer to his own shoulder and poured the contents of the flask through the livid lips.

"He lives!" cried Schneider.

The evidence was a faint flutter of the eyelids, a twitching of fingers and labored breathing.

Henri unrolled the blanket that served as a backrest, made a pillow of the wounded soldier's knapsack, and Schneider shifted his burden to this new resting place.

It was not long until the vigorous first aid rendered by the aviators found a more marked response—the heretofore unconscious officer looked up at the anxious faces of the workers, and perceptibly smiled through the beard that concealed his mouth.

He had comprehended that he did not owe a Russian for the help that had come to him in this extremity.

Schneider addressed him in the familiar tongue of the Fatherland, and Henri also added a word of sympathy and encouragement in the same tongue, at the time bending his head in the hope of a word in reply.

That word was spoken, and others in faltering train.

"He says his name is Schwimmer, Johann Schwimmer—captain."

"A captain without a regiment," was Schneider's sad comment, his eyes bending further afield, where corpses in blue, in heaps and singly, marked the path of deadly artillery practice.

"It does look as if we are caring for the only survivor," said Henri, realizing that Schneider's mournful observation was founded upon fact.

That Captain Schwimmer understood what was passing between his rescuers was manifest, for stoic though he was, he covered his eyes with a trembling hand and his breast heaved convulsively.

At the moment there was a startling diversion— the whip-like crack of rifles from the opposite edge of the bowl, at the very point where the aviators had stood when first attracted by the shining point on the captain's tunic.

Spat, spat—bullets boring the earth close to the right, left, and at the very feet of the trio on the ridge.

Schneider, again a firebrand without sentiment, coolly unslung the carbine from his shoulder, and put a shot across that evidently counted, for it raised a death-yell.

Without further ado, the soldier-airman plumped down on the ground, with his back to the sufferer on the blanket, and hoisted upon his broad shoulders the sorely wounded soldier, who faintly protested, and urged Schneider not to so hamper himself.

But you might as well argue with the wind; the sorrel-top warrior was up and away, making little of his load, Henri sprinting at his heels.

The firing company of Russians, either stragglers from the rear of a corps or scouts in advance of one, had evidently no intention of permitting the escape of several prospective prisoners, and they took up the chase as eagerly as the sporting pursuers of a deer, whooping and shooting as they bounded in a body across the separating hollow.

But for the good start made, Schneider could not have possibly, extra-weighted as he was, maintained speed enough to have gained even the base of the mountain for which he was heading. As it resulted, the carrier and the carried had hardly reached the first level, some fifty feet up, when the Muscovite marksmen were in close target range, and a leaden pellet among the many flattening against the rocks clipped the visor of Henri's cap as he cast a last look at the oncoming crowd before climbing like a squirrel into the rocky shelter above.

Schneider had placed Captain Schwimmer out of any possible line of fire from below, and was doing some return shooting on his own account. Unluckily for this style of defense, all of the surplus ammunition was in the locker of the biplane back in the woods, and the few rounds in the aviator's pockets were soon exhausted.

Henri knew that such was the situation by the fervid remarks of his companion.

But such was the angle of the aviators' perch that there could be no attack except from the front, and even that was a climbing approach.

It occurred to Henri, considering the lay of the land, that lead was not the only effective substance with which to repel boarders.

The ground was loaded with natural ammunition —loose rocks and rocks, thousands of them, from fist size up to a ton.

"Hey, old scout," hailed the boy, "give them a dose of dornicks."

Schneider took the hint with a burst of approbation.

"Two heads are better than one," he facetiously declared, hauling off his greatcoat for greater freedom as a heaver.

A dozen or more of the pursuing party were working up the acute elevation when the first huge stone thundered down the incline. The boulder made as clean a sweep as a well-placed ball in a bunch of ninepins.

"A ten-strike!" whooped Schneider. "Set 'em up again in the other alley!"

The Russians back-tracked for a time, finding a better range to fire at the defenders on the mountainside, and such was the fusillade that Schneider and Henri were compelled to stay in cover to save their skins.

"They can't work that game, though, to support a scaling force," said Schneider, "for the same fire would catch the scalers. If they come any nearer we can fix them, all right. But what a mercy it is that they haven't a field gun with them."

"As it is, we can't stave them off very long," added Henri. "When it gets dark the stone-rolling game won't work."

"Let me tell you, young man, when that hour comes, all they'll find here will be an empty nest."

The veteran had a moving plan up his sleeve, and the chief reason he had for making this stand was to give the injured captain a little more time to mend.

A scalp wound was what had laid the officer low, and since recovering consciousness he had rallied remarkably. In the soldier's knapsack, which Henri had thoughtfully carried, notwithstanding the hasty leave-taking, was three days' rations, and the invalid had also been strengthened by the food his new friends prevailed upon him to swallow.

During the day Schneider several times checked an effort of their foes to reach the height by starting a little avalanche of rocks at the critical moment.

In the periods of enforced peace, he cast an eye about for a likely way for quick retreat.

The way presented itself in the shape of a fallen pine that bridged a narrow pass, deeply dividing this isolated level from the mountain chain that widely extended back of the occupied position, and rose in serried crags to the very skyline.

It was a nerve-testing prospect, alluring alone to a professional rope walker.

"We'll tackle it in short order," resolutely declared Schneider, after final survey.

CHAPTER XVIII.

TRAILS THAT CROSSED.

When the biplane bearing Chief Roque and Billy Barry cleared the mountain top, the pilot and observer had a fixed understanding that every Russian camp was to be given a wide berth, for with fuel tanks going dry it would have been the top of folly to invite a long chase from the Muscovite airmen. And then, too, it was no part of a safe and sane program to risk an enforced descent in hostile domain.

"Keep her nose southward," commanded Roque, "and we may find the Austrian lines before we have lost our power. It's a desperate chance, of course, but there is nothing else to be done."

A precious hour was consumed in fruitless flight, with never a cheering sign of the friendly forces sought by the anxious aviators.

"It has just dawned upon me that our army has again entrenched in the mountains, for we could not possibly have come so far in the open without a single sight that would encourage further search in this direction."

Roque trained his glasses to the east, where the

snow-capped peaks of the Carpathians were showing in the dim distance.

"It's a good forty miles in that turn," figured
Billy, "and whether we can make it or not with an
inch or two of petrol is a close guess."

"Make a try for it, and count on the wind to
help."

The mind of the chief was set on this last throw.

One satisfaction to Billy in this change of course
was the definite objective—hit or miss, they were
no longer wandering.

Within a mile of the first slope the pilot knew that
the jig was up with the motors. Over his shoulder,
he called to the observer:

"This is no Zeppelin with a gas range, and it's
the turf for us now."

The motors clanked and ceased to hum. The
aëroplane took the downshoot and skated to a
standstill on the slippery soil.

"Stranded but not wrecked."

Roque accepted the inevitable with fairly good
grace for him.

"What's the next move?"

Billy was curious to know what the chief had in
stock for the emergency.

The boy was not immediately enlightened, for
Roque evidently proposed to reach speech through
meditation. The secret agent with his long coat-
tail dusted the powdery snow from a flat stone and

calmly took his ease behind the glowing tip of a long cigar.

"He must have wireless communication with a tobacco shop," thought Billy, "for he never fails to find one of those black rolls when he reaches for it."

The young pilot, muffled in a blanket, stuck to his seat in the biplane. It was his fortune, however, to see the first rift in their clouded luck.

The color scheme of the mountain side, brown, white and gray, added in the passing minute some new and stirring effects. On a higher slope were arrayed a number of men wearing crest helmets, blue jackets and red trousers.

"Say, boss," drawled Billy, when he caught sight of these gorgeous figures, "there's a circus band coming down the mountains."

Roque looked up. "Austrian dragoons!" he exclaimed. "We've rung the bell this time!"

Whether or not the dragoons heard Roque's exultant remarks, they were, nevertheless, gazing at and pointing to the spot where the stranded aviators were joyfully anticipating discovery. Willing to aid it, indeed, upstanding and waving welcome.

The soldiers came in haste to size up the strangely arrived visitors, and the leader recognized Roque as an oft-seen mixer in official circles. In calling him by name, however, the name was not "Roque."

The secret agent promptly explained the situation, and received hearty assurance that he could have enough petrol to carry him back to Berlin, if he wanted that much.

"We have fifteen air cruisers with us," stated the dragoon spokesman. "By the way, who is your pilot? You must have plucked him young."

Billy, notwithstanding Henri's patient instruction, was a little short yet in the Teuton tongue, but he had picked out of the conversation at this stage enough to put him wise to the fact that he was in the limelight.

"A bud as to years, I'll admit, my dear lieutenant, but in genius, skill and daring a full flower; one of the master craftsmen of the flying profession, and I left a companion piece on the other side of the mountain."

Threading Roque's eloquent tribute no doubt was the memory of that most recent rescue performance of the Boy Aviators in the black pass of Uzsok.

The boy from Bangor felt like the bashful member of a graduating class when the dragoons committed friendly assault by slapping him between the shoulders.

"Roten will steal you," laughingly predicted one of them. Billy later discovered that Roten was the chief aviator at army headquarters.

It was decided by Roque that Billy and himself should rejoin Henri and Schneider at once, the re-united party returning together to this camp, and remaining until the development of new plans of the secret agent.

Roten suggested that as it was the intent of the aviation corps to inaugurate a reconnoitering expedition the following day, it would be of mutual pleasure and benefit to combine in the trip.   Further, he advised Roque of a much more direct route over the mountains than the roundabout way uncertainly taken by the secret agent in coming.

"Consent"—this ready acceptance by Roque.

The army air scouts who were to participate in the expedition numbered eight, and the No. 3 piloted by Billy would measure speed with four of the swiftest biplanes in this branch of the service.

To the east of the Uzsok pass the Russians had constructed an elaborate network of cement and earthwork trenches, and to make any headway against the vigorous Muscovite defense at this point the Austrian troops would encounter a particularly difficult task.

It was up to the Austrian aviation corps to determine the true strength of the position, and to weigh the chances of an assault with the present artillery equipment in support.

So it happened that the little fleet was going in just the right direction to enable Roque to reunite his own party, at the same time affording him the opportunity to see for himself what was going on.

Roten had been fully advised of the exact location in the pass of the forest tract where Schneider and Henri were supposed to be watching for the return of their companions.

"We will find it without fail," he confidently declared, "and taking the nearest way there."

A blinding snowstorm, beginning in the night, served to hold the aviators in shelter for another day. At the first sign of clearing weather, however, Roten decided to fly, though he explained that many landmarks would be lost sight of under the drifts, markings recorded during a previous journey.

"Follow the compass, old man."

This remark, ventured by one of the lieutenants, the chief airman ignored with a sniff.

"Pass the word to pull out," he snapped.

Five biplanes were off at the signal, and winging their way in perfect alignment. As far as vision extended billows upon billows of snow capped the mountaintops and billows and billows of it smothered the defiles. The observers shaded their eyes as best they could with their hoods from the trying color effect, heightened by the reflection of the sun, and many times the pilots made hasty swipes with coat cuffs to dry wet cheeks.

Roten changed the course more than once during the first hour out, indicating that he was missing here and there some familiar formation that would aid the keeping of undeviating progress.

"We ought to get to the jumping-off place pretty soon at fifty miles an hour."

Billy felt that he had to say something to break the sailing monotony.

If Roque had an opinion he kept it to himself.

There was one thing sure, the flight had carried the aviators beyond the path of the recent blizzard, for brown and gray were again showing above the white in the checkered landscape.

That Roten was planning an intermission was apparent by the circling action of his machine over a plateau of broad expanse, probably an intermediate station with which he was acquainted.

His initiative set the balance of the flock on the down grade, and the pilots rejoiced over the immediate prospect of a thaw-out.

The chief aviator wore a satisfied smile on his bewhiskered countenance. "The Carpathians were never built to down me," he briskly proclaimed; "we'll go to the mark now like a bullet through cheese as soon as the steering boys get the cricks out of their backs."

"Come to think of it," volunteered Billy, "it is a tolerably nifty morning to hold a still curve for a hundred and twenty minutes at a stretch."

Roten, who understood American, grinned appreciatively at this recognition of his welfare action in behalf of the pilots.

"Right over there, Mr. Roque," he continued, indicating a summit a quarter of a mile distant, "is a rise exactly on a line west from where you started the other day to hunt for petrol—some twenty miles or thereabouts."

"You ought to have a medal for accuracy, my friend," genially complimented Roque, "and I apologize for holding the suspicion at least once to-day that the snow had thrown you out of balance."

"Can't blame you much, sir; I was mizzled a bit by too much white shroud back there. But here comes Ansel with the oil stove and the coffee pot, and we will have a brew that will reach all the cold spots under the vest."

"You must have been born for this kind of business," piped Billy, viewing the food display on a blanket laid like a tablecloth and the steaming coffee pot topping the little camp stove.

"I have had some experience in living in and out of an aëroplane," modestly admitted Roten, "yet I have seen days when I wished that I hadn't been born for this profession; hungry days, never-resting days, ever-perilous days. A sailor may be saved from shipwreck, a soldier has a fighting chance on the ground, but when an aëroplane goes too far wrong, just save the pieces, that's all."

"Right you are, sir," earnestly declared Billy; "but get it in the blood once and there's no quitting."

"By the way, speaking of military aviation, and

the cold we have endured to-day, it is no more a question of climate in that sort of work. Why, Russia is away up in the hundreds in the number of its aircraft."

"I expect that is true, Mr. Roque; I know I have met a few from over there myself," grimly conceded Roten.

"Perhaps some that you will never meet again," suggested the secret agent.

"Perhaps," said the veteran airman, reputed to have been mixed up in as many air duels as there were weeks in the year.

Billy, chumming it with Ansel, Roten's pilot, had challenged the new friend for a footrace, which led the runners to the edge of the plateau on the north.

Looking across the intervening defile, their attention was attracted by a movement on the opposite slope, the first sign of life below observed since they took flight from the Austrian camp early that morning.

"There is something doing over there," panted Billy, not yet recovered from the exertion of beating his companion a foot or two in their speed contest.

"I can't tell what it is, though," replied Ansel in broken English.

"It might be a bear," surmised Billy.

"More than one bear, then," claimed the Austrian,

"for I just saw two of the kind between the bushes."

"Your eyes are the better," conceded the boy; "there are two, one with a big hump on its back. I wish we could get over there."

Ansel shook his head. "You can't cross there on foot. Too deep."

"We can chase back and get the glasses anyhow."

Billy was already on the way for the means of satisfying his curiosity.

When the boy had secured the glasses and was hastening by the group around the little stove, Roque hailed him.

"What are you up to now?"

"Just going to take a pike at some mountain freak on the other side of the gully."

"Wait a minute, young man; I'll come and see what you have started." Roque carried a big bump of curiosity under his cap.

In the meantime, Ansel had told Roten about the slope climbers, whatever they were, and the aviation leader concluded that any sort of investigation on this trip required his presence.

The whole company, then, trailed after Billy across the plateau, with a general view of deciding in force the value of the alleged discovery.

From the lookout point a battery of glasses were soon trained upon the slope designated by Billy and Ansel.

Roten hit the moving mark first this time.

"I'll be blest," he ejaculated, behind the steady aim of the binocle, "if it isn't one big man carrying another on his shoulders, and a shorter fellow bringing up the rear!"

CHAPTER XIX.

RABBIT'S FOOT FOR LUCK.

For an hour the Russians in front of the rocky rise, where Schneider and Henri stood sentinel over the prostrate Austrian officer, had maintained an ominous silence.

Not a shot had been fired in the mentioned time, and no opportunity had been afforded the champion stone roller to make another ten-strike in repulsing attack.

"You can put it in your pipe and smoke it that this brooding over there means no good to us."

While Henri was not addicted to the pipe, he accepted the figure of speech, and fully agreed with his companion that the calm had sinister portent.

"The minute is about ripe," he volunteered, "for us to make ourselves scarce."

That Schneider was in accord with the proposition had evidence in the action of removing his boots. To cross a cavity that lowered two hundred feet or more on the unstable and untried support of a fallen pine warranted every precaution. There could be no crawling for the venturesome bricktop. He had human freight to carry on his back.

"Sorry to disturb you, captain," he apologized to the invalid soldier, "but it has to be done."

Henri, keeping watch at the front, sounded a note of alarm:

"Quick! I see what they're doing—it's a spread, and a three-cornered charge—they've stolen to the bushes right and left, and the firing gang in the middle is prepared to pot us if we show head or hand!"

Schneider bent to the task of lifting Schwimmer, the latter groaning at the movement.

Henri, balanced by Schneider's boots thonged over one shoulder and the knapsack swinging from the other, made a dash for the slender bridge. He had determined to first essay the perilous passage, and test the solidity required to bear the fourfold weight that would follow.

A single misstep, and for the error maker there yawned a pit of death, a mangling on jagged rocks lashed by the ice-laden rush of a brawling mountain stream.

But, sure-footed as the native chamois, with never a falter nor a backward look, the boy made the crossing, backed against the mound of upturned earth in which the roots of the fallen pine were imbedded, and fixed apprehensive eyes upon the burdened Schneider bravely and steadily advancing over the shaking bridge. Once the boy fancied that, with the earth clods tumbling from the mound behind, the whole structure was about to give, and he instinctively reached out for what would have been a vain endeavor to prevent the threatened disaster.

A moment later, with mingled sighs of exertion and relief, the man and boy clasped hands—on solid ground once more. The wounded officer had not realized other than that he suffered by the necessary lifting of his nerve-racked body.

Hardly a second, though, for the silent congratulation. On the level the defenders had just quitted in such thrilling manner swarmed Russian pursuers, seeking with fierce activity those who had conducted baffling resistance for several hours.

"Hear them yell," said Henri in suppressed tone.

"It's a sound better for the distance."

As Schneider made this comment he set shoulder against the root-threaded mound that anchored the fallen pine. With cracking of straining sinew the powerful pusher put every ounce of his wonderful strength into the effort of dislodgment. Thrice he failed, and then, with a tearing, grinding give, the mass loosened; another heave, and, as the perspiring giant threw himself backward, just escaping the void, the great trunk left its moorings and crashed with a tremendous shower of soil and stone into the abyss.

Schneider in a jiffy, and breathing like a porpoise,

dragged on his boots, again picked up the feebly remonstrating captain, and led Henri a merry chase around a rocky bend into the bush-grown level tabled between this and the next mountainous range.

Finally halting, and now beyond hearing of the whoops of the discomfited Russians, apprised of the escape of their prey by the crashing fall of the old pine, Schneider indulged in a cheer on his own account.

"Tough sledding, my boy, but a clean pair of heels to the gentlemen with the sheepskin overcoats. I don't know what's coming next, yet we can count on a 'next' coming."

Henri had to put in a sad word, owing to the depletion of the food store—the knapsack contained less than two days' rations for one man.

The eyes of the two aviators met in meaning glance—meaning that the remaining food should all be reserved for the ailing soldier, now sleeping quietly in his blanket roll.

Many a time in the hours of weary tramping did the aviators tighten their belts, but without a single utterance of complaint or bemoaning of sad fate. To the gnawings of hunger happily were not added the torments of thirst. Snow and ice served that desire.

The rations were sparingly fed to the invalid, who, unsuspicious of the sacrifice of his slowly starving companions, appeared to be gaining a measure of strength. He expressed sorrow that he must so burden Schneider in the march, noting that the latter had begun to occasionally stumble and stagger under the load.

"Don't you bother a bit, captain," as often assured the valiant aviator, "we will run into a friendly camp before long, and you will be in fighting trim before the moon changes again."

On the quiet to Henri, however, the big fellow confided that rest hours must lengthen if he had to fare much farther as a carrier.

He had discovered that in one of his revolvers there were still two cartridges that had not been exploded, and this find was due to the intention of throwing away these weapons as useless and cumbersome and a lucky farewell inspection of the long-possessed arms.

Schneider was a famous shot, with these same pistols had won several trophies, and, too, in war service had with them seldom failed to stop an antagonist lusting for his own life.

"Two bullets and three human lives at stake," he mused, weighing the revolver in his right hand, and aiming it at some imaginary living target. Several times during the day both Henri and himself had noted hare tracks in the snow, and Schneider even talked in a hopeful way of rigging up some sort of trap in the night. While the boy was inclined to be doubtful as to their possible success as trappers, under the circumstances, he did not spoil sport, in the mind of his companion, by adverse argument.

Now there was something tangible in the anticipation that Schneider might stalk and shoot a rabbit, and so hearten the weakened wayfarers to renew the battle for existence. They were beginning to lag with every additional mile traversed.

"Here is a good place to rest," announced Henri, whose sharp eyes had marked the mouth of a cave among the bushes covering the sides of the ridge, along which line the footsore travelers had been continuously plodding for an hour or more.

"We can't stop too quick to suit me," said Schneider, easing his living burden to the ground.

The cave was shallow, but ample in dimensions for the three invaders, clean and dry, and containing a quantity of dried moss.

Comfortably placing the invalid, Schneider dropped like a log in his tracks. He was completely exhausted, and knew no more of discomfort or the waking world until roused by Henri vigorously tugging at his coat sleeve. "There's game in sight," excitedly whispered the boy, "bring your revolver; crawl, and don't make any noise!"

The suddenly awakened sleeper rubbed his eyes, and, comprehending what was wanted, instantly produced the trusty shooting iron, and as quickly crawled to the mouth of the cave. Henri pointed a trembling hand to the little clearing a few yards below them.

Several hares, pure white, were hopping about, scratching and burrowing in the brown loam, there free of snow.

Schneider had for a second an attack of nerves, similar to that fever in the amateur Nimrod when first blundering upon the wallow of a buck deer.

Henri gave the shaking marksman a poke in the ribs.

"Shoot, old scout, or give me the gun!"

By the poke and the hissed demand, Schneider was himself again.

He drew bead on the nearest hare, and with the puff of smoke from the revolver muzzle the little animal made a frantic leap, ending in a complete somersault and an inert heap of fur. Another whiplike crack—and over went a second rabbit, stopped on the first jump to cover.

"Another cartridge or two and I would have potted the lot," boasted Schneider, "but even a pair of them is a mighty big draw for us."

Henri missed these remarks, for he was Johnny-on-the-spot to retrieve the game.

The pistol practice had startled Captain Schwimmer from a doze, and he was under impression that his friends were fighting off another attack by the Russians. The captain had begun to take notice of and interest in what was going on about him.

Raising himself on his elbows, he saw the result of the shooting match in the pair of plump bunnies swinging across Henri's shoulder when the boy capered into the cave.

It occurred to the captain to inspect the knapsack upon which his head had been pillowed. "Is this all the food in the camp?" he questioned, handling the few scraps in the sack.

Henri nodded in the affirmative, taken unawares by the quick query.

"And I have been eating my fill regularly on this march, have I not?"

"I hope you have not been hungry, captain," evaded Henri, realizing that the officer was putting two and two together.

"I see it all now," exclaimed the invalid, "you two have starved yourselves that I might live."

"Shucks, captain, don't put it that way: the rations were yours in the first place, and, besides, look at the glorious feast we're all going to have."

Henri's attempt to lightly pass the soldier's revolt against the self-denial practiced by Schneider and himself resulted only in the invalid turning face downward on the nearly empty knapsack, his emotion shown by convulsive movement between the shoulders.

Schneider, wise unto himself, had kept out of the discussion, and had practically contributed to the settlement of the hunger question by neatly skinning and cleaning the hare meat.

A hasty fire of dried moss and twigs and Schneider's big knife utilized as a spit raised a savory odor in the cave, and the picking of one set of bones that evening helped a lot to revive courage and hope. The captain, "by the doctor's orders," was compelled to accept his share.

The other hare made the breakfast for the third day out. Schneider alleged that he had a hunch that this rabbit business had turned the scale of luck, and to insure the belief he carefully pocketed the left hind foot of one of the animals.

During the morning the pedestrians, rested and fed, moved in fine style for the first few miles, Schneider stoutly holding to the efficacy of a rabbit's foot as a luck producer.

At the foot of the summit finally cutting off the level over which the party had been so long traveling, it was in order to do some climbing.

"It will give us a chance to look around," cheerfully observed Henri, "and which chance isn't coming to us down here."

Halfway up the height the boy was again heard from. He insisted that he had seen a flock of eagles in the western sky.

"Eagles your foot," bantered Schneider; "whoever saw a flock of eagles?"

"Wild geese, then," insisted Henri.

"How many did you see?" quizzed Schneider.

"Five or six, maybe."

"Guess again," laughed the big fellow; "geese would be lonesome if that was all in a flight."

"Have it any way you please; I suppose you will be claiming next that I am suffering with liver spots."

Henri was a bit nettled that Schneider did not take seriously his sky story.

About twenty minutes later, Henri called another halt. "Now, old scout," he cried triumphantly, "just look up for yourself and say what you would call 'em."

Schneider, shading his eyes under a hand, scanned the blue expanse above. "By the great hornspoon," he almost shouted, "I believe they're aëroplanes!"

Henri was more than willing to be convinced that such was the fact.

"What do you think about it, captain?"

Schwimmer had from the first joined in the sky-gazing contest.

"I think our friend Schneider has solved the problem. I never saw a real bird with exactly that motion."

The blots on the sky were increasing in size.

"It's a sure thing," hurrahed Henri, "and they're circling for a landing!"

"Perhaps they're Russians," mildly suggested the captain.

"Not while I'm carrying this rabbit's foot," firmly asserted Schneider.

CHAPTER XX.

WINNING OF THE IRON CROSS.

The aviators in the party of Roten were all for sailing, post-haste, to the slope where the mysterious climbers had been sighted, and very shortly the little fleet was in the air, headed that way.

Flying low, the observers kept a sharp lookout for the near appearance of the man with the burden and the "shorter fellow."

Roque caught the first glimpse, and called to his pilot to risk a look for himself. Billy had only a side glance, as the machine rounded the summit, but that was enough for him.

"It's Henri and Schneider, or their ghosts!" he shouted.

Roque fixed his glasses for the close view.

"As sure as shooting it is, but how in the world did they get here?"

Billy had no ear for this—he was for landing right there, even with a chance of plowing through the bushes. However, reason ruled, and he steered for a clearing, into which the biplane promptly plumped.

Hardly waiting until the machine had run its length, the boy was out and speeding to greet his chum.

It was a regular collision, the manner in which the youngsters came together.

"Glory be!"   This was Billy's high-pitched note.

"Here's to you, Buddy, bully old boy!" Henri cried.

The "bully old boy" then made a dash for Schneider and worked the latter's brawny arm up and down like a pump handle.

Roque repeated the last-named performance with both the recovered members of his crew.

In the meantime the Austrians were saluting Captain Schwimmer, well known to them as a gallant officer in a famous command.

"But for them, gentlemen," gravely stated the captain, nodding toward Schneider and Henri, "I had been in my last fight. Through danger, cold and hunger have they brought me, and neither needs a patent of nobility—nature took care of that."

Roque had only to listen to the happy reunion chatter of the boys to get the side of the story he wanted to hear.

"It seems," he commented, "that Billy and I were not in the same class this time with these trouble hunters."

"Do you suppose that there is anything left of our biplane?"

Henri had taken on the air of a sea captain who had lost his ship.

"That is an important question," said Roque. "There is only one fit mate to that craft in this part of the country."

Fortunately for the preservation of good feeling, Roten did not hear this latter statement.

It was necessary to detail two corporal aviators to take the wounded captain back to army headquarters, where he could have the skilled surgical attention that would hasten his recovery.

As the invalid was lifted into the machine that was to do ambulance service, he gave a hand each to Henri and Schneider.

"From my heart I thank you both," were his last words in profoundly earnest farewell.

Henri traveled as a passenger with Billy and Roque in the brief journey to the forest station in the pass where it was hoped to find intact the stranded biplane.

Schneider, who had been given a lift by Roten in the trip, was in high glee when it developed that the No. 3, behind its screen of bushes, had sustained no damage.

"See that?" The big fellow held aloft the rabbit's foot. "There's no jinx that can beat it."

Roque was delighted to learn, as the aërial expedition proceeded, that one of his cherished desires had matured—a large German contingent had arrived to support the determined effort of the Austrian forces to relieve the Przemysl fortress.

He had made up his mind that it was well worth the risk to carry back the new word of hope to the hemmed in garrison, and Roten was informed of his purpose.

"I regret that you must quit us, Mr. Roque," said the aviation chief, "but it's the big thing you are going to do, and I certainly wish the best for your undertaking. Let me advise, however, that not a screw should be loose when you make that dash. You can't fall in that country now without bumping a Russian."

"I'll back my boys to make the riffle," confidently asserted Roque.

"They'll need the keen eye every inch of the way," persisted Roten.

"We came out safely, and I guess we can repeat," declared the secret agent.

"Well, good-bye, sir, and look out for the big guns at Malkovista; the Russians are there now, and it's only three miles from Przemysl."

"We've come into our own again." Billy and Henri were standing together, viewing with satisfaction the graceful lines of the No. 3's, every part adjusted to a nicety. Both boys were well aware that they were to run a through express.

Schneider had been supplied by a brother aviator with a new outfit of firearms, and, as usual, was spoiling for an uproar.

"Going, going, gone." His imitation of an auctioneer was excellent, and with this send-off the biplanes bolted for Przemysl.

The pilots themselves knew the route this time, and they sent the biplanes over the course at sixty miles an hour.

Three times they were over the fire of long-range guns, but too high for harm.

Settling in the fortress enclosure, their initial greeting came from Stanislaws.

"Here's a cure for sore eyes."

This delighted individual capered around the welcome incomers like a dancing master.

The garrison received with acclaim the news that Roque conveyed.

They had been advised in a general way by wireless from the nearest Austrian point of the upcoming of the German reinforcements, and this confirmation in person and in detail added to the enthusiasm created by the first report.

"Now, boys," said Roque to his pilots, the next evening, "I am seeking a sight of the gray lines again, and there's another hard flight in store for you. So get a good night's rest. We start at daybreak."

Facing a bitter, biting wind, the aviators left

Przemysl at dawn, and when they, numbed but un-
daunted, finally reached the far-away German lines
it was a battle front that they crossed. There the
atmosphere was being warmed by gunpowder
flashes, and below was burning petrol, thawing out
the ground that the troops might dig themselves in.

Before the entrenchments, in wide range, combined forces of Austrians and Germans were locked
in a life and death struggle with Russian con-
tenders for the possession of Warsaw—a bloody
repetition in one spot of the never ending conflict.

Though completing a continuous flight of seven
hours, the aviators were there offered no tempta-
tion to alight. Hovering over the banks of the
Bzura they saw a German cavalry detachment all
but totally destroyed by the exploding of a Russian
mine, and in turn the big guns of the Germans cut
wide swathes in the Muscovite ranks.

Schneider cheered or groaned as the tide of battle swept forward and back, when victory favored
or defeat menaced his comrades in the fray. The
firebrand, in every quivering fiber, madly craved
the chance to brave the shot and shell on the black-
ened battlefield.

He saw a German color bearer go down in the
press of a hand-to-hand conflict, and as the mass
was dissolved by artillery fire, that one still figure,
among the many scattered in the open, presented
irresistible appeal to the soldier-aviator.

"Land me, boy—have you the red blood to do it? Have you the courage, lad? You have, I know. Do it, lad—do it now!"

With his incoherent address, the big observer spasmodically clutched the shoulders of the young pilot.

Carried away by the vehement pleading of the man behind him, Henri set the planes for a straight fall.

Schneider bounded from the skimming machine, made it the work of a few seconds to reach the flag, which the dead man had wrapped around his body, and as quickly returned.

The powerful motors drove the biplane up and across the field, with the colors trailing over the shoulders of the observer, who, in his excitement, sang a mighty war song.

This deed of daring, directly in view of the trenches, and under the very eye of the German commander and staff, raised a tremendous cheer.

Of all this Schneider seemed oblivious. His was a blind patriotism.

Roque wore a look of mild reproach when he encountered Henri behind the lines that night, but he could not resist the prompting of forgiving admiration when Schneider stood before him in attitude of apology.

"Had no orders, of course, boss, but something stuck to my crazybone, and everything went."

"You will have something stuck on the breast of your coat, or I am very much mistaken," said Roque, extending his hand, which Schneider grasped with fervor.

That "something" was to be the Iron Cross, the famous decoration for valorous service, and the most coveted distinction in the German empire, a badge of courage woven into its military history.

"Were this boy a soldier of and for the Fatherland," solemnly continued Roque, "the royal gift might well be bestowed upon him."

Schneider threw an arm around the shoulders of the young aviator. "Of nothing else is he lacking to claim the honor," feelingly maintained the big fellow, and his eyes were moist as he spoke.

Henri shook his head. Then with a roguish glance at his chum, he said:

"The only medal I am hankering after is the one Billy and I are expecting for making the first aëroplane flight across the Atlantic."

"Have the 'made in Germany' mark on your machine and I believe you can establish the record," laughed Roque.

"Not on your life," exclaimed Billy. "We are going to build the crossing craft ourselves."

The No. 3's were lying idle behind the lines. Roque had ceased overground work for the time being, and like a mole was engaged in some un-

dermining scheme, of which the boys had no inkling.

Resorting to his remarkable aptitude as a lightning change artist, and also applying the magic
touch to Schneider, the pair of them were scarcely
recognizable to even the lads with whom they had
been so long and so closely associated.

The secret agent and his trusty lieutenant were
masquerading as natives of Russian Poland, and
it may be told that their desperate mission was
to enter Warsaw, where the slightest indiscretion
or betrayal would put them in graves alongside of
that daring spy of Roque's who failed to conceal
his identity.

It was the midnight hour when Billy was awakened by a man enveloped from neck to foot in a
grayish-brown overcoat, from under the head cape
of which came the voice of Roque:

"Take this" (slipping a fold of coarse paper into
the hand of the drowsy lad), "and if you do not
hear from me after three days, read what is writ-
ten, and follow the instructions to the letter. Not
a look at the message, remember, for three days; to
be exact, the morning of the fourth day. You hear
me?" Billy sleepily nodded his head.

Out on the turbid tide of the yellow river beyond the German trenches two shrouded figures
silently launched a flatboat and drifted away in the
darkness.

"What's doing?" This was Henri's morning question, preceding a swallow of coffee.

"If I knew what was in here I could probably tell you a whole lot that I don't know at present."

Billy displayed the closely folded packet containing Roque's instructions.

When Henri was advised of the conditions imposed he accepted the trust as a matter of course.

It had never been a habit of the boys to break faith.

CHAPTER XXI.

HELD IN WARSAW.

THE din of battle had long since ceased to be an inspiration of terror with the Boy Aviators. They were case-hardened by continual contact with the war game, and too careless, perhaps, of flying lead.

Reclining in the trenches, they indulged in all sorts of surmises as to the whereabouts of Roque and Schneider, wagered back and forth, one way and the other, on the proposition of whether the chief would appear in person within the allotted time or put it up to them to interpret the message in Billy's pocket.

With the passing of two days, the hours in the next one seemed to move on leaden wings.

"I don't even know in what direction to look

for his coming," complained Henri. "If he is coming," he corrected himself.

"No use getting in a stew about it," advised Billy, concealing the fact that he himself was nearing the boiling point as the last few hours of waiting wore away.

The morning of the fourth day, and no sign or sight of the absentees.

Billy and Henri sat in council, and the former opened the paper that had haunted his dreams during the previous restless night.

"If alive, we are in Warsaw."

"I guessed that once."   Billy lifted his eyes from the paper.

"Go on," impatiently urged Henri.

"Of either fact you may learn by following instructions.   You are to bring both biplanes, early morning, and circle over the city.   In the south section you will note tall column with figure on top in center of square.   Back of same is elevation on which rise two towers.   Watch these.   If one flag shows, hold over high road running west; if two flags, sail north and land at lodge house where canary sang for us.   There wait.   If highroad route (one flag), see red scarf signal for drop.   When you read and commit these lines destroy."

"What a system that old fox controls," observed the reader. "Killing one of his men didn't close the show in Warsaw. Do you get all this, pard?"

"I think I do," asserted Henri, "but let me go over it again to be sure."

Both boys having Roque's communication pat in their minds, Billy tossed it into the flames of the nearest campfire.

The aviation lieutenant serving with the division gave them free reign and all possible assistance in preparing for their flight. He asked no questions.

Crossing the river, the young aviators ascended to great altitude, hardly visible to any casual ground view, and taking lower levels gradually over the city. Each with an eye on the compass, the pilots mentally rehearsed their instructions.

Operating in unison, though a hundred yards or more apart, they checked speed when sighting the burnished tower tops showing above all other structures on the south line, first identified by the tall column and its surmounting statue in the square.

The aërial maneuvering continued for a seeming quarter of an hour, and while the sun rays splintered on the glistening turrets over which they were keeping vigil, no other manifestation appeared.

Through this long exposure to the danger of attracting unwelcome attention, the boys were momentarily expecting some aëroplane demonstration

from the Russian military camps showing to the
east.

On the highroad, finally, the aviators saw two
horsemen galloping their mounts towards the hill,
and then lost to view between the twin bases of
the towers.

A flag swung out from one of the tiny windows
under the gilded domes.

One flag:

The signal to hold over the road, which stretched
whitely for a mile or more and merged into the
fertile fields without the city.

The red scarf next. Would it call the suspended
biplanes in swift swoop to the earth?

Skilled hands gripped the levers in readiness to
instantly respond to the signal.

A cart with two muffled figures in it rumbled
leisurely down the road. There was no urging of
the sorry steed straining at its belled collar.

The biplanes perceptibly lowered, though it was
merely guess work on the part of the aviators. The
movement of the cart might have been just one of
ordinary traffic, the occupants just plain, everyday
peasants.

Suddenly the hovering airmen got a signal, but
not the expected flash of scarlet. One of the
carters, a big fellow, rose from his seat and fran-
tically waved his arms, and the boys were then so
near that they could plainly see that he varied the

queer performance by pointing skyward with the long whip he was holding.

So intent had been the aviators in trailing the cart that they had neglected for a time to look elsewhere about them.

The gestures of apparent warning that they were witnessing returned their wits to normal, and what they had from the first low flight feared was about to be realized. Barely a half mile away, and buzzing toward them, were three aëroplanes, which, unnoticed by the otherwise engaged lads, had risen from the Russian camp.

Billy and Henri, now wholly confident that the antics that had awakened them to the impending peril were those of no other than Schneider, gave that good friend a parting salute of cap waving and turned about at full speed to lead a stern chase over and beyond the city—far beyond, it proved.

The pursuing biplanes, of the largest type, carried a crew of three men each, and that they had tremendous motor power was evidenced by their catapult coming.

But, light-weighted, the No. 3's were not to be easily overhauled. It must have been a contrary spirit that induced Billy and Henri to do other than head across the river to the German camp.

They were in their element, however, and it was the kind of exploiting that most appealed to them. Keeping out of range of the guns of their armed pursuers was the first care, and no other care had the lads how long the chase continued.

They would even hold, as a bait to keep the fun going. That grave consequences might follow capture was not at all an issue. The boys had no thought of aught else than that they were jockeying in an aëroplane race.

How far afield they had driven they did not realize until with waning day they had outdistanced their pursuers.

They were compelled to land in strange territory, for they feared to take the chance of exhausting the supply of petrol carried by the aëroplanes, and, besides, the continued strain on the aviators themselves was beginning to tell.

"Oh, for a 'lodge in some vast wilderness,'" spouted Billy in actor style. He had a very pleasant memory of that lodgekeeper's kitchen, in which they, cold and hungry, had been warmed and fed. "I'd like mighty well," he added, "to hear that canary twitter right now."

"Barring all that," remarked Henri, "we might be in a worse fix, considering that we have something to eat with us and a good pair of blankets for a bed."

"I am not particularly impressed with these surroundings, though," argued Billy, "a swamp on one side, a bunch of stunted willows on the other, and a regular no man's land front and back."

"Oh, quit your kicking, Buddy, and let's make the best of it."

Henri started for the willows, in the hope of finding enough dry material to make a fire.

He succeeded in coaxing a small blaze out of a little pile of twigs.

Dead tired, the boys rolled into their blankets and slept like logs. But they had a rude awakening, particularly in the case of Billy.

As he lay snoring, a flash more vivid than lightning dragged him out of dreamland, and his hands flew to his eyes to protect them from the blinding glare. A searchlight was playing full on his face. He heard the clatter of horses' hoofs, and before he could see what was happening, a hand was on his shoulder and a revolver was pressed against his breast.

Henri, startled into sitting posture, looked dazedly upon the proceedings.

A Russian cavalryman, dismounted, was behind the revolver, and the searchlight was directed from a wagon.

A stalwart figure in gold and brown, an officer in the service of the Czar, moved briskly into the circle of light to inspect the prisoners.

Stroking his tawny mustache, he concluded brief comment with a short laugh. Translated, what he said was:

"You have caught a pair of lambs, Peter."

The soldier addressed as Peter hastily restored the revolver to his belt.

Another soldier just then discovered the biplanes, and the officer deemed this find of great importance. He tried the French language on the boys in starting a series of blunt questions.

"Who and what are you?" he demanded.

"Aviators by profession, foreigners by birth, and prisoners because we couldn't help ourselves."

The officer smiled at Henri's smart answer.

"I suppose you came to this spot in those machines?"

"Yes, sir," replied Henri, less snappy in tone.

"We will hear more from you when we get to Warsaw," advised the Russian.

"Shades of Tom Walker," thought Henri, " 'out of the frying pan into the fire.' "

"Peter and I will go along with you by the air route," proposed the officer; "I like the looks of those machines. We need them. Now, Peter, you must not let your pilot run away with you."

Peter grinned and tapped the butt of his revolver.

Captain Neva, for such was the Russian officer's title and name, was a rather advanced amateur in knowledge of aircraft, and he shrewdly estimated the value of the prizes that had come to his hand on this night's march. The subaltern, Peter, had also some flying experience, though he preferred a good horse under him rather than a board, and he, too, noted the fine points of the No. 3's.

"A pretty present for the general, my captain," he rejoiced, "and all ready for delivery."

The boys were given a substantial breakfast, and Henri learned that they were about 150 miles north of Warsaw. As this was figured on straight line measurement, the aviators realized that in the excitement of yesterday's racing they must have left the direct course many times, for considering the time they were in the air and the speed maintained, 150 miles was not a great distance.

From one of the many wagons, loaded with ammunition and military supplies of all sorts, was produced a fresh supply of petrol for the biplanes.

"You see, we have quite a number of these flying machines up in Warsaw," explained Captain Neva to Henri, "and we are carrying plenty of this stuff to feed them."

In a few minutes the biplanes were off for Warsaw, Henri and the captain in one machine, Billy and Peter in the other.

Three hours later the boys walked behind the captain into army headquarters, and soon into the presence of a man of most distinguished bearing, in full field uniform of a Russian general. Though gold lace sparkled on his shoulders and his cuffs, the striking note of his attire was the orange and black ribbon of the Cross of St. George that appeared along the buttoned edge of his field coat.

Captain Neva presented the compliments of his colonel, told of the near approach of the supply wagons and convoying troops, and mentioned the handsome addition to the aërial fleet so luckily and peculiarly acquired. The captain's brief relation of the latter incident, a little break in the pall of war, seemed to interest the general, for he glanced at the lads, standing at respectful attention nearby.

"What is your name?" he asked, speaking in French, and looking directly at Henri.

The boy politely bowed and named himself.

"I would conclude from the sound that I have spoken in a tongue within your complete understanding. And the other?"

Henri registered Billy, name and nation.

The boy from Bangor flushed with gratification when the general, in excellent American, called him forward.

"You're a long way from home, young man."

Billy admitted the fact, and added, "I have been wishing many times of late, sir, that the distance could be reduced three-fourths and I had already traveled the other fourth."

With the incoming of the staff members, reporting from the front, the general consigned the boys for the present to the custody of Captain Neva.

"They've wasted no time," observed Billy, pointing to the familiar lines of the No. 3's, glistening with new color.

That a couple of Polish carters should happen to be gaping at the aviation show was not an unusual occurrence or usually worthy of notice.

But there are carters and carters, and some seeming carters are not carters at all!

CHAPTER XXII.

AN HOUR TOO SOON.

WITH incoming of the troops convoying the supply train, Captain Neva rejoined his company, and Billy and Henri were promptly adopted by the aviation corps, most of whom spoke both French and English, and all very much inclined to express their admiration of the aëroplane knowledge displayed by the youngsters.

The boys were right on the job, so to speak, when it came to reassembling the parts of new aircraft received by wagon shipment, and so grew in the confidence of the aviation lieutenants that they were quite often permitted to make flying tests of the various machines with only themselves in charge.

If the young airmen enjoyed this concession without watching on the part of the lieutenants, there was no such inattention on the part of a couple of frequenters of a city tavern not far removed from the aviation camp.

Work was evidently slack with this pair of citizens, for hardly a day passed that they did not spend several hours at a tavern table located near a bow-window, which afforded an excellent view of the parade ground and aviation quarters.

One of these constant spectators was remarkable for his size and the vivid hue of his hair, the other for the reason that he paid absolutely no heed to the other patrons of the place, though all appeared to be of his kind, both in manner and attire.

On a particular afternoon, the strangely silent one was deeply engaged with a stump of a pencil in the labor, no doubt, of casting up his accounts on a piece of dirty brown paper, in which had been wrapped his lunch of black bread and sausage.

The puckered lines over his nose indicated thought labor, but the furtively keen glance he occasionally gave to outside movement contradicted the impression that he was of slow order of mind.

The chief actors in the mentioned "outside movement" at the time were two trimly set up lads in new suits of service green, one pulling and the other pushing an armored biplane into its hangar.

"This machine," said the puller, "ran like an ice-wagon to-day but maybe use will smooth her out."

"It's all in the motors," confidently asserted the

pusher, "and I'll have the kinks out of them in a day or two."

The man at the table across the way had completed his task, shoved the paper and pencil into his pocket, and was placidly puffing a huge cigar.

His red-topped companion stamped into the room, returning from some excursion in the city, but the smoker did not pass a word of greeting, though the other idlers filled in with noisy welcome.

It was not until the room had been vacated by all but themselves that the curiously assorted pair put their heads together.

"Ricker showed you where the ammunition was stored?"

The red-topped nodded.

"You arranged for the plans with Westrich?"

Again the nod of assent, but this time with softly spoken supplement:

"All good, but there is no chance of us getting to the river now. It's lined with a wall of steel, and even a rat could not pass, day or night, without a triple stamp of authority on its back. And let me tell you, if we light the match for that explosion without an outlet, all the information we will carry will be to the next world."

"If we cannot get through the wall of steel you mention there might be a way of going over it."

The speaker gave a meaning glance out of the window at the aviation camp. A biplane was just rising for test flight, and it was manned by two experts easily identified by the conspiring couple in the tavern.

"Oh, ho, I see," mused the brick-top, "you expect to use those boys in the matter of pulling us out."

"Why not? Have they ever failed us in extremity? Is the peril greater than when they dived into the canyon that our lease on life might be lengthened; did they fail to respond to my summons to do this very work of rescue, delayed through no fault on their part?"

This subject had served to draw the clam out of his shell, and he found relief in relaxing temporarily his studied pose of stolid indifference.

"How are we going to get at them?" asked the willing listener to the rapid-fire praise of the young heroes.

The crafty secret agent (it was Roque, of course) had not been wool-gathering during the silent hour of his sitting at the table.

He had devised several ways of apprising the boys that he needed their services and acquainting them with a working plan that would enable them all to sail out of Warsaw in safety.

Something was going to happen when he willed it that would make the outward passage a memorable one, and success or complete failure of the project was in the close balance of a few more hours.

In real truth, however, Roque did not so greatly weigh his personal welfare as against the service he could render by doing damage to the foe from without as well as from within.

Ready for his call were papers of supreme import, and to lose which at the hands of a searching party would be a calamity the secret agent dreaded even to anticipate.

By the air route he had determined to leave, if by any hook or crook Schneider and himself could get hold of an aëroplane.

Billy and Henri had been aloft for several hours, enjoying a bird's-eye view of the really magnificent city, for the possession of which carnage held sway for hundreds of miles.

"Some town this," Billy remarked as he stepped from the machine, completing the sightseeing tour; "after the war I'd like to start a branch factory here."

"Oh, go 'way," laughed Henri, "it would take a derrick to haul you out of Boston or Bangor, once you set foot again in those burgs."

"You forget, old top," suggested Billy, "that we have already on tap a comeback aëroplane trip across the Atlantic. I'm no quitter."

From a coal-laden wagon the contents was being shot into a chute running into the cellar of one of the big houses taken over for officers' occupancy.

One of the grimy heavers, at sight of the boys,

came forward to meet them, wiping his hands on the leather apron he wore, removed his fur cap, and took therefrom a scrap of smutty brown paper and tendered it to Billy.

"Guess he wants you to sign a receipt," said Henri, looking over his chum's shoulder.

Billy's glance at the paper set him staring at the man who presented it.

The latter never raised his eyes—he was using them sidewise upon a group of soldiers standing in front of the mess hall.

The boys saw in the scrawl these words: "Orders for No. 3's, Two Towers, St. Michael road, eight sharp, Thursday evening."

Without a word, Billy returned the paper to the heaver. The officer of the day was approaching. He signed the delivery receipt, but the paper had queerly changed color in the handling.

As the lads slowly walked toward aviation headquarters their minds were all in a whirl. Prisoners they were and prisoners they had been, yet in both instances it had been but the semblance of captivity. While they were held, the rein had been a loose one.

Just back of them the ties of long association, immediately in front of them a trust imposed, a generous parole, when they had gone to the limit in giving the best of themselves, in the one capacity they could serve, to the former rule.

Thursday evening at eight, and this was Tuesday evening at six. Long enough, indeed, for the boys to torment themselves with the reflection that if they did not appear at the appointed hour Roque and Schneider would curse their perfidy, and if they did betray the confidence of the aviation chief in this camp he would pay the penalty.

"It will be no trick at all to take the biplanes for an evening spin; we have done it before without question."

"That's the trouble, Henri," lamented Billy, "it's too easy. If we had to steal the machines, risk our lives before the guns of the sentries, and all that sort of thing, it wouldn't seem such a trial of conscience. But they take us on trust, and without question."

"Yet, here's Roque and Schneider in the lurch, and looking to us for aid. With them we have met about all that is coming to a fellow in this war zone, except death, and pretty near that; we have eaten and slept and starved together."

"There you are again, Henri, and it's 'twixt the devil and the deep blue sea!' any way you put it."

Thursday morning, and as clear as a bell. The Boy Aviators looked red-eyed on the smile of nature. Their cots had squeaked protest all through the night against the tossing of the uneasy nappers.

At noon they had about made up their minds to keep the appointment at Two Towers, and seeking to strengthen this resolution they avoided in every way they could meetings with the aviation chief.

Along about three in the afternoon the wavering youngsters had arranged a compromise, this to be positive. They would deliver the No. 3's to their former owner for choice, and so enable their old friends to get safely away. As for themselves, they proposed to return to camp and "take their medicine"—their dose and the portion that the aviation chief would otherwise be likely to get

But fate shuffled it another way.

The workday was in the closing minutes. The remaining city thousands who were not in military service were swelling the stream of homegoers in the busy streets.

The driver of a coal wagon, which had drawn up before an imposing structure devoted to the storage of army supplies, and supposed to contain an immense supply of ammunition, suddenly conceived the notion that he was doing overtime duty. At least such was his manner when one of the Big Ben clocks overhead ding-donged the hour of six. Perhaps, too, the movement of gathering up reins and whip had its measure of prompting in the appearance of the driver's mate from some underground space in the big building.

At any rate, the old nags dragging the heavy vehicle were given the full benefit, and without warning, of a long and knotted whip-lash, and covered several city blocks at a lively gait before they realized that they were traveling out of their class.

The heaver who had emerged from the building in response to the clock summons showed tremor of the hands when he lifted them to draw the cape of his greatcoat closer about his throat.

"It's set for eight," he hoarsely whispered; "I turned the key when I heard the strokes outside."

Strangely enough, the wagon kept a course directly to a residence section at once fashionable and quiet, and hardly the possible location of a coal yard or the home, either, of a humble employee thereof.

One of the men in the wagon, the fellow with the hoarse whisper, left the vehicle in a square marked by a tall column with a statue on top, while the driver continued the urging of his horses up the ever ascending street.

Gaining the level above, the horses were given their own heads, which meant a snail's pace. Close at hand were two towers of considerable height.

While the horses plodded on the highroad stretching to the west, pressure on their bits was lacking. The wagon was empty.

Two figures appeared on the terrace back of the twin towers, these terraces rising in tiers from the bank of the fast-flowing river below.

"You left Ricker in the square?" This question

put by the man who evidently had just returned from a mission that did not include a ride in a coal wagon.

"He left me, rather," replied the late driver, with a touch of grim humor.

The first speaker held a watch in his hand, consulting it frequently, holding it closer and closer to his eyes as the light faded before the advance of night's shadows.

"Seven o'clock," he announced. "Another hour."

This was the last notation of time by the watch holder.

There was an explosion that, notwithstanding the distance, seemed to shake the everlasting hills to their very foundations.

The men on the terrace stared aghast, each at the other.

"The die is cast," cried the one with the commanding voice, "and an hour too soon!"

CHAPTER XXIII.

A LEAP FOR LIBERTY.

THE Boy Aviators had just left the mess hall, and were proceeding to the hangars where the No. 3's were housed, fully intending to carry out their compromise plan of giving Roque and Schneider the means to escape, and return themselves as hostages for the honor of the aviation chief.

Shortly before seven o'clock on this eventful evening, Billy and Henri had the biplanes in order for the arranged visit to St. Michael road, and the delivery of one or both of the machines to their former owner, supposedly in waiting in the shadow of the two towers.

"It is really a relief that the time is drawing nigh for us to get off the rack. I believe we are doing the square thing, but sure we have had few easy moments during these last forty-eight hours."

Billy heaved a sigh when reviewing this disturbing experience.

Henri turned just then to salute the aviation chief. The boy's greeting had none of the cheery note usually there. He did not know how it would be several hours hence.

"Looks like a chance for you boys on the next dispatch trip to Petrograd," advised the chief; "we can illy spare more than two at a time of our regular air scouts, and here's a deal by which we have two extra machines and a pair of pilots thrown in."

With their minds clear and no cloud like the one looming ahead, the prospect of biplaning to the wonder city of Russia would have set the boys on the top floor of enthusiasm.

As it was, they could only say that they would welcome the work if it should be assigned to them.

The aviation chief had hardly taken a dozen steps in his continuing round of inspection when there was a shakeup that might have come by a combination of volcano and earthquake.

"Geeminy!" gasped Billy, clapping his hands to his ears, "somebody must have fired a ton of powder!"

A roll of drums preceded the hasty assembling of several regiments in this division, and a squadron of cavalry jingled madly down the street.

"That was a whopper, all right," exclaimed Henri, righting himself after his first little stagger from the shock, "but big noises ought not to queer us, pard. Get in and get away."

Following his chum's example, Billy was close behind the former in upward flight.

They could see that the streets below held literally surging masses of humanity, all trending in the same direction.

The aviators speedily gained an idea of what had happened. That which only the other day they had observed as a solid front of granite and iron on a building covering practically a whole city square had fallen in ruins, completely blockading the broad avenue it had faced.

About the square a cordon had been drawn, and it could be seen, even through the dusk, that troops were spreading fan-shape from this point throughout the entire northern section, while the police darted right and left and everywhere.

The select neighborhood of St. Michael road had not been omitted from the general round-up, the boys found, when they approached the site of the two towers.

It seemed that the abandoned team and wagon had been found somewhere along the highroad, and as suspicion was now acute, the discovery set the fine-comb going along every terrace and police poking in every likely hiding-place.

There had been instant acceptance of the theory that the storehouse and magazine had been deliberately blown up by the cunning contrivance of a spy or spies within the city.

Every stranger must give an account of himself, and even some individuals here and there who were not newcomers.

Billy and Henri could see no opening where two full length military biplanes could alight without notice, and not a morsel of encouragement to try for negotiation on the quiet with the disguised secret agent who had summoned them.

But the aviators hung about, not knowing what else to do for the present, thinking that Roque would make a showing of some sort, as he usually did in tight places.

Flying lower and lower, the two biplanes were sweeping within earshot of the terraced heights along the river front, and though now of dim vision, searching parties could be seen flashing lights up and down the ground tiers.

There was a hullabaloo breaking out on the lowest terrace, immediately overhanging the river—a shot—another and another—like a bunch of firecrackers, so fast did they follow!

A stentorian note of defiance, a rush, two shapes springing out into space, a great splash in the icy waters below!

If the morning revealed a single trace of the daring fugitives dead or alive, no word of it reached the aviation camp, to which the young airmen had returned, conscious that of this mission they were acquitted.

"Do you know, I can't help believing that they got across?"

Henri had a thought, perhaps, of the rabbit's foot that Schneider carried.

The boys had many under-the-breath discussions as to the possible connection of Roque with the explosion that had destroyed the war depot. They had no reckoning that in the little shop of a silversmith, not far removed from the very column and statue that had twice served them as a guide-post, the whole story might have been told by a wily confederate posing as a peaceful artisan. This same man could also have confessed to the first error of his expert career in the handling of a time-clock.

With plots and counterplots, however, the young aviators had no time or inclination to meddle. They would rather work in the open.

"I wonder if that lieutenant meant what he said about giving us a peek at Petrograd?"

Billy put the question to his chum as they contemplated with satisfaction a particularly neat job of aëroplane repair they had just completed.

"Don't see why he should say it if he did not mean it," replied Henri. "Next time he comes this way there would be no harm in reminding him of what he said."

It so happened that the aviation chief at the very moment was headed for the hangars. He was accompanied by two officers of apparent high rank, who gave the various types of aircraft close and critical inspection.

When the No. 3's came to their notice, one of the officers, a grizzled veteran, with a livid scar showing from temple to chin, halted with a pointed word of commendation.

"There's speed, balance and strength for you. Where were they built?"

The aviation chief explained.

"Ah, I see," said the officer, "the paint only is ours. Well, I think we need look no further. Get them ready for immediate use. Where are the pilots for this assignment?"

A call was passed for Billy and Henri.

When they faced the official visitors, both of the latter turned a stare full of question marks at the aviation chief.

"Are these the sons of our pilots to be?"

The senior colonel meant to be a bit sarcastic.

"No; but if the fathers really were as remarkably skilled in the high art of aëroplaning as 'the sons' you see here, I would request the general to let me go after them without delay."

The airman was very much in earnest in his firm but respectful effort to correct the impression of his superiors in command that he had been guilty of some error of judgment.

Henri unconsciously contributed another entering wedge when he gave his name to the younger of the colonels, who had taken a hand in the examination of the youthful candidates proposed by the aviation lieutenant for special aëroplane service.

"Trouville!" exclaimed the officer; "are you of the house founded by the first François and the motto 'Sans Peur'?" (Without Fear.)

"That's in my family record, sir," admitted Henri, who could not imagine what on earth his ancestry had to do with his ability to run an aëroplane.

"Then you will find an open door in Petrograd," proclaimed the colonel, "that of my father, who in his day of travel was often a guest at the Château

Trouville, when your grandfather lived and they were kindred spirits in the world of art."

"Château Trouville and its art treasures are no more," sadly recalled Henri.

"My father will mourn with you there," assured the colonel.

Another assurance came from the aviation chief when the officers had returned to army headquarters to assist in the preparation of dispatches that were to go forward by aëroplane within the hour. Said the lieutenant:

"It is settled, my flying friends, that you are to go on this journey, which is imperative, owing to the investment of railroad connections. The observers behind you will point out the route, and easy to follow, as the river is ever in sight. As to the rest, you need no instructions."

"We are ready to start at the drop of a hat, sir," declared Billy. The boys had tuned the No. 3's to the point of perfection.

The observers and dispatch bearers, Marovitch and Salisky, honor men in the service, soon appeared, hooded and enveloped in furs.

The first named handed Henri a card. "From Colonel Malinkoff," he said. The boy saw that it contained the words "He is a Trouville," signed "Alexander," and directing to a certain street and number in Petrograd. Henri carefully pocketed the valuable reference.

In the early afternoon the young aviators had their first view of the capital city of the Russians, at the mouth of the Neva, and they made landing upon a massive granite quay on the south bank of the big river.

As the boys walked with the special messengers to Admiralty Place, they marveled at the colossal proportions of the public buildings, and looking up and down one magnificent avenue, five or six miles in length and 130 feet wide, Billy squeezed the elbow of his comrade, with the awed comment: "There's all outdoors in that street."

"That's the Nevskoi Prospekt," advised Marovitch.

"The very name on the colonel's card," cried Henri, "Malinkoff palace, too."

"Know it very well," put in Salisky, "a twenty-minute ride, and you are there."

When the dispatches were delivered the boys were not present, but there was no lack of interest for them outside. Standing near the copper-inlaid doors through which the messengers had passed were a number of Cossacks, dressed in scarlet, gold-braided caftans, white waistcoats and blue trousers.

"That's a fancy looking bunch," whispered Billy; "I guess they are something extra. And— say, Buddy, if my eyes don't deceive me that fellow in the middle, the one with the bushiest beard,

is no other than the boss of the crowd who shoved
us in the cellar over in Galicia!"

"Cracky, what a pair of eyes you've got, old
scout, and sure it's the very same, though he doesn't
look as rusty as he did then."

Henri seemed to be fascinated by the discovery,
and watched like a hawk every movement of the
old enemy in the new garb.

About that time the Cossack happened to cast
a glance in the direction of the spot where the boys
were stationed, and two pairs of eyes met in a single
flash. In the fierce orbs, and under the beetling
eyebrows of the knight of the mountains and des-
erts, the flash plainly conveyed a puzzled expression. Henri lowered his look. This risk of recognition was more than he intended his bid to bring.

Turning away, the boy sought to show his indifference of the now strained situation. He managed
to get an aside to Billy, in effect:

"I'm afraid I've put my foot in it now."

With the reappearance of Marovitch and Salisky,
Henri, in subdued tone, requested information re-
garding their brilliantly attired neighbors.

"Why," responded Marovitch, "they are of the
personal escort of the Czar."

"Good-night," thought Henri, "it's a fix we are
into, and less than two hours in the town."

"How far did you say it was to the Malinkoff
palace?" he suddenly asked.

"Oh, about two miles up the Prospekt," said Salisky.

"Hail one of those carryalls, please," requested the aviator, pointing to the nearest stand of vehicles for hire.

The Cossack had followed them, and was slowly descending the marble steps just quitted by the boys and their companions. He was evidently still debating with himself.

The driver of the chartered vehicle cracked his whip and carried his passengers up the street as fast as his heavy horses could gallop.

With a speed ordinance he had no acquaintance.

CHAPTER XXIV.

AGAIN THEY WON OUT.

DRAWING up with a flourish in front of a most pretentious example of old-time architecture, the fur shrouded jehu reached for his fare, which matter was adjusted by Salisky, who had orders from his colonel to see the boys through from start to finish.

At the onyx-studded entrance of the palace the party was halted by a gorgeous flunky, who immediately unbent at a word from the useful Salisky.

"The colonel must belong up in the pictures

here," suggested Billy, duly impressed by the surroundings.

"He is a great noble as well as a great soldier," reverently remarked Marovitch.

"Well," chuckled Billy, "I'm going to keep on my shoes, even though I walk on velvet."

Salisky gave the lad a side glance of disapproval of this levity, of which the young aviator took not the slightest notice.

But Billy warmed to the gracious presence revealed by cordial greeting in the spacious drawing-room.

The card from Colonel Malinkoff had preceded the visitors.

With Marovitch and Salisky in the background, the boys were ushered forward to meet a real, live duke, but, withal, a kindly gentleman without a mark or an affectation of exalted rank.

"Which, may I ask, is the Trouville, the grandson of my old friend?"

Henri bowed acceptance of the honor. With fine and delicate courtesy Billy was made to feel that he was not counted a crowd by being the third participant in a cozy chat.

The duke delighted in his memories of the close alliance he had maintained with the house of Trouville, and received with extreme regret the information that the old château had been razed by the engines of war.

"I well remember the underground passages, the walled ways, the secret panels, and the like of the ancient place."

Henri nudged his chum, and then briefly narrated how the fortune of the Trouvilles had been saved through the use of these same concealed avenues and by the plan of the same two boys now sitting in this drawing-room.

The old noble listened intently to the story, told without embellishment or boast, and at the point where Henri referred to the delivery of the treasure to his mother the duke clapped his hands in applause.

"Salisky," he called to the special messenger, "I desire to keep these young gentlemen as long as possible. Is there an emergency that commands their return?"

"Your grace," stated Salisky, "it grieves me to say that it is most important that they serve as pilots in our journey back to the front. Even now dispatches are being prepared, and we must be on the wing at sunrise to-morrow."

"Ah, the same duty that holds my son in its grip, the call of country, and which by my infirmity of years I may not answer. Not your country, my boy, but your trust, nevertheless. But this is not your last visit by many, I sincerely hope. A Trouville, a Trouville," he muttered, "without fear."

"Oh, another thought, you have not broken bread

with me." The duke struck a bell on the table at his side.

The gorgeous flunky led the way to the smaller of the dining-rooms, the other would have held a regiment, and if the food was plain, on the war basis of all alike, there was a bountiful service of it.

From the dining-room windows the Prospekt could be seen, and Henri saw something besides the Prospekt—several horsemen in parti-colored uniforms pacing their mounts slowly up and down in front of the palace.

He telegraphed with a wink to his chum, who was seated with his back to the windows. Billy took the tip, and managed to get an overshoulder look on his own account.

The interest of the boys as to affairs inside instantly began to flag. True, they were under powerful protection for the time being, but there was a later time coming.

The Cossack must have struck the lost chord in his memory. There had since the encounter in the Galician farmhouse been a life added to the claim of the red rider—the duelist that Schneider had forced over the cliff.

Henri had a game to play—playing for time. Appeal to their host, for various reasons, did not impress the boy as a desirable proceeding.

"There is no need of our going back to Admiralty

Place right away, is there, Salisky? We don't sail until morning and we haven't even seen the paintings here."

"The paintings"—here was a master stroke. The duke was touched at a point nearest his heart.

"You must have at least a passing look," he insisted.

Salisky uneasily shook his head. "We have orders to be within call from and after six o'clock, and, sir, it is already very near that hour."

"Now, I will tell you what to do, Salisky; you and your comrade here take my car, report yourselves, and if it then be necessary for my young friends to join you, return here for them. It is only the matter of a very few minutes, either way."

Protesting under his breath, Salisky and his companion heard the summons for the duke's automobile, and were whirled away in that swift conveyance.

They could not understand the action of a company of imperial Cossacks in ranging alongside of the machine, and only withdrawing when the indignant chauffeur sent the machine forward with a vicious plunge.

An hour passed, and no word from the departed special messengers.

The boys walked with the duke through his magnificent gallery, but it is doubtful if they had any high appreciation of the treat. In every picture they saw a Cossack wrapped in a rainbow.

Finally, observing their inattention, and attributing it to anxiety on their part at the committing of a breach of discipline, the duke instituted inquiry as to the whereabouts of his chauffeur, intending to forward the boys at once to Admiralty Place. Neither driver nor machine could be found on the premises.

Billy felt that it was his turn to get into the figuring.

"It is such a fine evening, sir, and a straight way, that, if it is all the same to you, Henri and I would like the exercise of walking back to headquarters."

Henri could not fathom the scheme that his chum was nursing, but he made no objection to the proposition.

The duke did not accompany the boys further than the door of the art gallery, stating, with a grim smile, that he had always with him a reminder of his fighting days in the shape of a "game leg." He gave them both a kindly farewell and exacted a mutual promise of a longer visit next time.

Behind the broad back of the flunky the lads proceeded as far as the drawing-room, when Billy "happened to think" that he had left his gloves in the dining-hall. There he looked for his missing gloves—out of the window!

In the glow of the high-lights on the broad avenue were revealed the gold-braided cavalrymen of the earlier hours, still patiently pacing their horses up and down in front of the palace.

"Tell his nobs to see if the automobile has arrived," softly urged Billy.

Henri sent the flunky ahead to investigate. He guessed now, and correctly, that his chum did not intend that they should leave by the front door.

Like ghosts they flitted through the dimly lighted corridors of the palace, into the unknown backstairs regions, hoping to find an easy outlet at the rear.

An open window coming handy, the boys essayed a jump therefrom, landing on all fours in the walk leading to the tradesman's gate. Darting out into a side street, the fugitives relapsed into a brisk walk, fearing to here excite suspicion by undue haste.

Alone in a great and strange city, as ignorant of locality as of the language spoken by the average inhabitant, Billy and Henri, as the former would have put it, "were up against it, good and strong."

Yet they won out, and meeting the wildly searching special messengers in the gray dawn, without ado climbed into the pilots' places of the waiting biplanes and sent the powerful machines in whirring flight toward the distant towers of Warsaw.

To follow them beyond this fixed destination is to turn the leaves of the next record, under the title of "Our Young Aëroplane Scouts in Russia; or, Lost on the Frozen Steppes."

THE END.